The Midnight Fox

FABER & FABER

has published children's books since 1929. Some of our very first publications included *Old Possum's Book of Practical Cats* by T. S. Eliot, starring the now world-famous Macavity, and *The Iron Man* by Ted Hughes. Our catalogue at the time said that 'it is by reading such books that children learn the difference between the shoddy and the genuine'. We still believe in the power of reading to transform children's lives.

The Midnight Fox

BETSY BYARS

ILLUSTRATED BY MARTIN SALISBURY

FABER & FABER

This edition first published in 2014
First published in 1968
by Faber & Faber Limited
Bloomsbury House, 74–77 Great Russell Street
London, WC1B 3DA

Designed and typeset by Crow Books
Printed and bound by CPI Group (UK) Ltd, Croydon, CR0 4YY

A CIP record for this book is available from the British Library

ISBN 978–0–571–31942–8

FSC
www.fsc.org
MIX
Paper from
responsible sources
FSC® C101712

2 4 6 8 10 9 7 5 3 1

ABOUT THE AUTHOR

Betsy Byars was born in North Carolina, USA. Her father worked in a cotton mill, and Betsy went to school in a cotton-mill village. Her early aspirations were to work with animals, but then she married an engineering lecturer and moved to Illinois. Housebound with young children, Betsy began writing articles for newspapers and magazines. As the children started to read, so she began to write stories for them. Using her own children's experience, and memories from her own childhood, she produced many children's books. She now lives in South Carolina.

One

Bad News

Sometimes at night when the rain is beating against the windows of my room, I think about that summer on the farm. It has been five years, but when I close my eyes I am once again by the creek watching the black fox come leaping over the green, green grass. She is as light and free as the wind, exactly as she was the first time I saw her.

Or sometimes it is that last terrible night, and I am standing beneath the oak tree with the rain beating against me. The lightning flashes, the world is turned white for a moment, and I see everything as it was – the broken lock, the empty cage, the small tracks disappearing into the rain. Then it seems to me that I can hear, as plainly as I heard it that August night, above the rain, beyond the years, the high, clear bark of the midnight fox.

To begin with, I did not want to go to the farm. I was perfectly happy at home. I remember I was sitting at the desk in my room and I had a brand-new $1.98 Cessna 180 model. I was just taking off the cellophane when my mom came in. I was feeling good because I had the model, and all evening to work on it, and then my mom told me in an excited way that I was going to Aunt Millie's farm for two whole months. I felt terrible.

'I don't want to go to any farm for two months,' I said.

'But, Tommy, why not?'

'Because I just don't want to.'

'Maybe you don't *now*,' my mom said, 'but after you think about it for a bit, you will. It's just that I've taken you by surprise. I probably shouldn't have come bursting in like –'

'I will never want to go.'

She looked at me with a puzzled shrug. 'I thought you would be so pleased.'

'Well, I'm not.'

'What's wrong?'

'There's nothing wrong. I would just hate to stay on a farm, that's all.'

'How do you know? You can't even remember Aunt Millie's farm. You don't know whether you'd like it now or not.'

'I know. I knew I wasn't going to like camp, and I didn't. I knew I wasn't going to like figs, and I don't. I knew I wasn't –'

'The trouble with you, Tommy, is that you don't *try* to like new things.'

'You shouldn't have to *try* to like things. You should just very easily, without even thinking about it all, *like* them.'

'All right,' she said, and her upper lip was beginning to get tight. 'When I first saw this farm, I very easily, without thinking about it at all, *loved* it. It is the prettiest farm I ever saw. It's in the hills and there are great big apple trees to climb and there are cows and horses and –'

'Animals hate me.'

'Tom, I have never heard anything so silly in my life. Animals do not hate you.'

'They do. How about that dog that came running up at about a hundred miles an hour and bit me for no reason? I suppose that dog loved me!'

'The lady explained that. The dog had a little ham bone and you stepped on it and the dog thought you were going to take it. Anyway,' she continued quickly, 'just wait till you see the baby lambs. There is nothing dearer in the world. They are –'

'I'll probably be the only kid in the world to be stampeded to death by a bunch of baby lambs.'

'Tom!'

'I tell you, animals don't like me. Perfectly strange animals come charging at me all the time.'

My mom ignored this and went on about the fun I would have in the garden, and especially gathering eggs. There was, according to her, no such fun in the world as going out to the henhouse, sticking your hand under some strange hen, grabbing an egg, and running back to the house with it for breakfast. I could picture that. I would be running to the house with my egg, see, having all this fun, and then there would be a noise like a freight train behind me. A terrible noise growing louder and louder, and I would look around and there would come about two hundred chickens running me down. CHAROOOOOM! Me flattened on the ground while the lead hen snatches the egg from my crushed hand and returns in triumph to the coop.

My mom could see I wasn't listening to her, so she stopped talking about the fun and said, 'I should think, Tom, that even if you do not particularly want to go to the farm –'

'I don't want to go at all.'

'– even if you do not *particularly* want to go to the farm,' she continued patiently, 'you would realise how much this trip means to your father and me. It is the only chance we will ever have to go to Europe. The only chance.'

My mom and dad were going to Europe with about fifty other very athletic people, and they were going to bicycle through five countries and sleep in fields and barns. You can see that parents who would do that could never understand someone not wanting to go to the farm. I could not understand it myself completely. I just knew that I did not want to go, that I would never want to go, and that if I had to go, I would hate, loathe, and despise every minute of it.

'Don't you want your father and me to have this trip?'

'Yes.'

'You're not acting like it.'

'I *want* you to have the trip. I want you to have a hundred trips if you want them, just as long as I don't have to go to any crummy farm.'

'You make it sound like a punishment.'

'Why can't I stay here?'

'Because there's no one for you to stay with,' she said.

'There's Mrs Albergotti.' This shows how desperate I was. Mrs Albergotti was the kind of sitter who would come in the room where I was sleeping to see if I was still breathing.

'Mrs Albergotti cannot stay with you for two months.'

'Why not?'

'Because she has a family of her own. Now, Tom, will you be reasonable? You are not a baby any more. You are almost ten years old.'

'I am being reasonable.'

My mother looked at me for a long time without saying anything. I lifted the lid off my model box. Usually this was a great moment for me. It was usually so great that trumpets should have blown – TA-DAAAAAAA! This time I looked down at the grey plastic pieces and they were just grey plastic pieces.

'Your father will talk to you when he gets home,' she said, and left the room. I could hear her cross the hall into her room and shut the door. My mom cried easily. The week before we had been watching a TV show about an old elephant who couldn't do his circus routine any more, and suddenly I heard a terrible sob, and I looked over and it was my mom crying about the old elephant. Well, we all laughed, and she laughed too, only it was not so funny to hear my mom crying now, not because of an old elephant, but because of me.

That evening my father came in and talked to me. My dad is a high-school coach who likes to tell about things like the Lehigh-Central basketball game, when he won the game in the last two seconds with a free throw. If anything, I knew that he would be less understanding than my mom. He had not understood, for example, why I did not want to be in Little League even after he had watched me strike out seventeen times straight.

'This is a wonderful opportunity,' my dad said enthusiastically. 'Wonderful! There's a pond there – did you know that? You can go swimming every day if you like.'

'I'm not much of a swimmer,' I reminded him. This was the understatement of the year. Having a body that would not float would be a great handicap to anybody.

'Well, you can learn! That is why this is such a wonderful opportunity.' Then he said earnestly, 'If you go to the farm with the right attitude, Tom, that's the main thing. With the right attitude, two months on a farm can make a world of difference in you both mentally and physically.'

'I like myself the way I am.' I continued working on my model, which was what I had been doing when this conversation started.

'Put down the model, son.'

I put down the model but kept it in my hands so he would know I was very eager for the conversation to be over.

'Son, this trip means a lot to your mother. She has never had a real vacation in her whole life. Remember last summer when we were all packed to go to the Smokies and you got the measles?'

'Yes.'

'And she stayed home and nursed you and never complained once about it, did she?'

'Well, no.'

'Now she has a chance for a real trip and I want her to have it. I want her to go to Europe and see everything she's wanted to see all her life. And I don't want her to be worried about you the whole time. As long as she thinks you don't want to go to the farm, she is going to worry.'

'But I *don't* want to go.'

My father sighed. 'You don't have to let her

11

know that. For once in your life you could think of someone besides yourself!'

Sometimes when my dad said something like that to me – well, I wouldn't actually cry or anything; my nose would just start to run. It did this all the time really. One time after school my teacher said, 'Tom, I am very disappointed in you. You simply are *not* working up to capacity this term.' Well, I wanted to tell her that I could not work up to capacity sometimes, the same as anybody else, that she need not expect me to be perfect just because my parents were teachers, only I couldn't say anything because my nose started to run.

Now, I put my hand up to my nose and said, 'All right, I *want* to go to the farm.' Then I picked up my model and started pretending to work, because my eyes were kind of wet too.

My father never knew when to leave me alone. Now was the time for him to say, 'Fine,' and walk out of the room. Instead he just stood there. After a minute he cleared his throat and said, 'You won't be sorry, son. You're doing a fine thing for your mother.'

Silence from me. Nose running worse than ever. Couldn't even see what pieces I was forcing together.

'And I bet – I just bet that you're going to have the time of your life on that farm. Millie says they've got some baby pigs. I bet you can have one.'

'I have always wanted a baby pig,' I said. I thought sure he would know I was being sarcastic, because *no one* has always wanted a baby pig. Maybe some farm girls would see one little pig that didn't look too bad and say, 'Hey, let's dress it up,' and they would play with it and feed it from a baby bottle, but no one has *always* wanted a baby pig.

But my father seemed pleased and clapped me on the back. 'Good going!' This was what he said to his players when one of them excelled. 'I'll tell your mother.' He went to the door, then paused and said carefully, 'I'll tell her you've changed your mind and are eager to go to the farm. Right?'

'Yes, tell her that.'

He went out and I wiped my nose and eyes and looked down at my model, which was practically ruined. I have never had less fun for $1.98 in my whole life.

Two

The Trouble with Leaving

The evening before I went to the farm, my friend Petie came over and we sat on the steps without saying anything. Usually we talked all the time, but that evening we just sat there and watched an ant on Petie's sneaker. Petie was transferring the ant from one sneaker to the other, crossing his legs all kinds of different ways, so that no matter which way the ant ran he was always on a sneaker. This ant must have thought, *Wow! There are one thousand boys in sneakers lined up here and I will never get to the end of them.*

Well, finally Petie got tired and let the ant get off his sneaker and run into the grass. I could just see that ant running home and his wife saying, 'Why, you must have had a terrible day. You look awful!'

And this ant says crossly, 'Well, you wouldn't look so good either if you had run across one thousand boys!'

Then Petie said, 'I wish *I* could go to the farm.'

'You don't either, Petie Burkis.'

'Well, I wish I could go to the same farm you're going to. It's not going to be so much fun here by myself, you know.'

'It'll be more fun than at the farm.'

'I guess, I saw this TV show about a farm one time,' Petie said, 'and this city kid comes to the farm for a visit and gets lost.'

'So what happened?'

'Well, fortunately for this city kid, Lassie lived on this farm, so somebody said, "Go find him, Lassie, go find the little lost city kid." '

'And did she find him?'

'Well, I turned to something else myself, but I think it's a pretty safe guess that she did.'

We sat in silence for a few minutes and then I said, 'I'll probably get lost on the farm.'

'You probably will.'

'Only there won't be any Lassie to come find *me*.'

'Yeah, but there'll probably be some other kind of animal, like a real smart horse –'

'Or a pig,' I said disgustedly.

'Yeah, there'll be a real smart little pig, and somebody will say, "Go find him, Piggie, go find the city kid," and Piggie will find you and the next day there'll be big headlines all over the world: BOY RESCUED FROM DEATH BY PIGGIE.' Petie was going to be a reporter when he grows up, so he was good at doing headlines. One time the teacher hit his hand with a ruler because he kept on tapping his desk after she asked him to stop, and he made up this headline – BOY DEALT CRIPPLING BLOW BY TEACHER – and then he went on to write a story that sounded like it really had come from a newspaper.

'Hey,' Petie said now, 'maybe you'll get to be on "I've Got a Secret" and your secret will be –'

'*I was rescued by a piggie*,' we said together.

'They'd guess it right away though. But you could still sell your story to *Life*.'

'Yeah.'

We didn't say anything then, because for a minute it had been like old times and we had forgotten that I had to go to the farm. Now we remembered and were quiet. Finally Petie said, 'Well, I have to go.'

'Aw, you don't have to.'

'I do, too. Mom said I could just come over for a minute to say goodbye, and I've been here for a couple of hours.'

'All right. Write to me, Petie.'

'Sure, only you better answer.'

'I will.'

'And tell me what the farm's like and if you have to milk cows or anything.'

'And you tell me what's going on around here.'

Petie kicked the pavement with his foot, and then he said, 'Well, so long,' and went down the street. I went in the house and sat down on the bed beside my suitcase, which was all packed so that we could get an early start in the morning.

I wished Petie had not mentioned that about milking the cows, because that was probably exactly what I'd have to do. My first chore.

'Run out and milk the cows, will you, Tommy?'

And they'd give me this enormous ten-gallon galvanised bucket and send me out, thinking that anybody with any sense at all would know how to milk an old cow.

And I would walk down to the barn, real slow, and this very beautiful cowboy's voice would start singing like in the movies when the cowboy hero is walking into town to meet his doom. And this cowboy's voice would describe all the awful things that were about to happen to me, and the camera would show me walking slowly to the barn with the enormous ten-gallon galvanised bucket hitting me on the leg.

I stopped thinking about that and put the two models my mom had given me into my suitcase. It was surprising that my mom, who was smart enough to teach school, could not pick out a decent model. One of these was a race car which had about six pieces and I had done the same one when I was in first grade. The other was a horse model which had to be painted and I did not like to paint.

I got undressed and into bed. I had not bothered to take my suitcase off the bed and my legs were real tight and cramped under the covers. Downstairs my mom said, 'I still can't believe it!' She had been saying this in a very happy and excited way all week. Then my dad said something I couldn't hear and she said, 'I know, but I still can't believe it.' I, lying upstairs with a ten-ton suitcase against my legs, found it very easy to believe.

To pass the time I began to count all the things I was going to miss by going to the farm. For one, some hornets had started building a nest on the shutter outside Petie's window and he was making a special invention so he could spy on the inside of the hornets' nest in complete safety. Also Petie's Aunt May knew a lady in Anderson who had a secret room in her house, and she had said that she would take us over there and let us see it, only we had to go this summer because they were going to tear the house down to make a new car park.

What I was going to miss most, though, were just everyday things that weren't planned at all. Like one time Petie and I found this awful-looking Kewpie doll's head, and Petie pretended to throw it away, only when I got ready for bed that night and turned down the covers, there was the Kewpie doll's head on my pillow staring up at me. So then, without saying a word, I took the Kewpie doll's head and secretly hid it in Petie's underwear drawer. Then he hung it on a string in my closet, so that it hit me in the face when I opened the door. And all the weeks we were hiding that Kewpie head, we never once mentioned it to each other. That's the kind of fun that doesn't sound like much when you tell it, but I would miss it on the farm.

Three

Abandoned

We left for the farm the next morning after breakfast. No one had much to say, so my mom turned on the radio and we listened to a disc jockey play hit songs from the past. About noon we stopped for a picnic lunch by a place that advertised candy, fireworks, toys, real arrowheads, flags, coins, and souvenirs from all fifty states. I used to like to spend hours looking at that kind of stuff, but that day I didn't even feel like going inside. Finally, after we ate, my dad said, 'Come on, sport, I'll buy you something,' so we went in and I selected a little totem pole that had been made in Japan, and then he made me get this fake plastic ice cube which had a fake fly in it and we went out and put it in Mom's cup for a joke. It was a very dismal morning.

The rest of the way I just sat in the back seat with my eyes closed. I started thinking about a movie I saw once where some farm people sent to the orphanage for a boy, because they wanted someone to help with the hard work on the farm. Instead of the boy, the orphanage sent them a puny girl, and there was tremendous disappointment. I thought now that perhaps Aunt Millie and Uncle Fred were letting me come because they thought I was a great athlete with muscles like potatoes who could toss hay into the loft without spilling a straw. They would be very excited, of course, at the thought of this wonderful summer helper, and as our car drove up, they would be standing in the yard saying things like 'Now we have someone to break the wild horses for us,' and 'Now we have someone to get the boulders out of the north forty.' Then I would step out and they would cry, 'But where's the *big* boy?' and I would say, 'I'm the only boy there is.' They would try to hide their disappointment, but finally Aunt Millie would start crying and run into the house.

I then went on to imagine a wonderful ending, where I turned out to be such a merry boy that I brightened the entire household, bringing fun to a dark house, but this didn't cheer me up, because it seemed to me that any farm people would rather have a sullen muscular worker than a skinny one, no matter how merry.

While I was thinking about this, we turned off on to the dirt road that led to the farm. My dad started blowing the horn to announce our arrival. When we got to the house, where the drive made a big circle and was all neatly edged with whitewashed stones, he called out, 'Anybody home?'

Right away Aunt Millie came running out of the house, drying her hands on her apron and shouting, 'Fred! Fred! They're here.'

I got out of the car – I never felt less muscular in my whole life except in gym class – but she was so busy hugging Mom that she didn't notice me.

'It's been so *long*!' she was saying.

My mom started crying and said, 'Oh, Millie, it is so *good* to see you. You are exactly the same, and this farm is exactly the same!' and then she cried some more.

'Now, Fran,' my dad said.

'And this is Tom,' Aunt Millie said, turning to me. She was not really my aunt but my second cousin, but I called her Aunt Millie, so I said, 'Hello, Aunt Millie. It's nice to see you.'

'Well, it's nice to see *you*. I'm so glad to have a boy around this place again. All my boys have grown up and gone, and it's lonesome.' She patted my shoulder, and then she turned back to Mom and said, 'Hazeline went riding with her boyfriend, but I *told* her to be back in time to see you. I said, "Hazeline, Fran has not seen you in years and you be home."'

'I still remember how fat and sweet she was when she was a baby,' Mom said.

'I guess you do. Why, you *were* her mamma that summer. Me flat on my back and you – she thought you *were* her mamma.'

My father had gotten my suitcase out while they were talking, and now we all went into the house and had lemonade and cake with Uncle Fred.

We talked some more about Hazeline, and Uncle Fred told about this prize pig of his, and Dad told some basketball stories, and then – it seemed like we had just been in the house about one second – my dad said, 'Fran, we are going to have to get started if we want to get home tonight.'

'You're not leaving!' Aunt Millie said. My feelings exactly.

'We have to.'

'But we wanted you at least to stay the night.'

'We can't. That's what we wanted to do,' Mom said, 'but the couple we're riding to New York with want to leave first thing in the morning. Tom says he doesn't mind, but I feel awful just dropping him and running.'

'Oh, now, Tom is going to get along fine, aren't you, Tom?'

'Sure.'

We walked out on the porch without saying anything, but at the steps Mom said, 'Now you be a real good boy, Tom, and do what Aunt Millie tells you.'

'I will.'

'We'll get on just fine,' Aunt Millie said, patting my shoulder again.

'I know.' Mom hugged Aunt Millie and said, 'This is the nicest thing that anyone has ever done for me.' Then she hugged me real hard, got into the car, and turned her face away.

My dad said, 'Well, so long, sport,' and socked me on the arm.

I said, 'Have a nice trip.' I was pleased that my nose wasn't running or anything, because I felt terrible.

My dad started the car and they drove off. Mom kept her head turned, but Dad waved and honked the horn all the way to the highway.

'Now, you watch,' Aunt Millie said. 'Hazeline and her boyfriend will come driving up in about ten minutes all full of apologies. I *told* her to be here. That girl! You want to come on back in the house and have some more lemonade?'

'No, I'll just walk around a little bit,' I said.

'Sure.'

She went back into the house and I sat on the steps. My dad was always talking about control. He said control was the most important thing there was to an athlete, and he was always telling me I should have more of it. I couldn't imagine anyone having more control than it took to sit quietly on the steps, nose and eyes dry, while being abandoned.

Sometimes my dad would get real disgusted with me because I didn't control myself too well. I used to cry pretty easily if I got hurt or if something was worrying me.

30

I remembered one time when Petie Burkis came over to my house and told me that he knew a way that you could figure out when you were going to die – the very day! He learned this from a sitter he'd had the night before. It was all according to the wrinkles in your hand – you counted them a certain way. Well, we sat right down and counted the wrinkles in my hand. It took over an hour, and it came out that I was going to die in my seventy-ninth year, on either the eighty-second or eighty-third day. Petie said probably I would fall terribly ill on the eighty-second and last until just after midnight on the eighty-third.

Then we started counting the wrinkles in Petie's hand. He had a peculiar hand, and it came out that he was going to die on the two hundred and seventy-ninth day of his ninth year. Well, Petie was nine years old right then, so he said, 'Get a calendar, quick, get a calendar,' and he looked like he was already getting sick.

We looked all over the house before we finally found a wallet-sized insurance calendar, and then we got down on our stomachs and began to count the days. We were saying the numbers together – two hundred and seventy-six, two hundred and seventy-seven, two hundred and seventy-eight – and I can still hear the terrible way it sounded when we both said, 'two hundred and seventy-nine.' It was like the last sound in the world, because it turned out that Petie was going to die the next Saturday.

I said, 'Let's do it again.'

We did it again, very slowly and carefully this time, but it still came out the same – two hundred and seventy-nine, next Saturday.

Petie felt awful, I could see that, and I felt even worse, and if there had been any way in the world I could give him nineteen or twenty of my seventy-nine years, I would have done it in a minute. He said, 'I better get home,' like he meant, 'before something happens,' and then he left and I was too upset to try and stop him. I went into the house and my mom said, 'What's wrong now?'

I said what was wrong was that Petie was going to die on Saturday, and right away she started laughing. I said, 'Well, I certainly wouldn't think it was so hilarious if *your* best friend was going to die this Saturday,' and I went out of the room.

She caught up with me in the hall and hugged me, and then she sat down on the telephone stool and made me look at her, and said, 'Tommy, Petie is *not* going to die this Saturday.'

'How do you know?'

'I just *know*, Tom.'

'How?'

'Well, look at him. He is in perfect health. He is absolutely the healthiest boy I know.'

'Healthy people are hit by cars every day, or fall down wells. You don't have to be sick to die.'

'This is some fool thing you and Petie have cooked up. I think you enjoy getting all worked up about nothing.'

'We do not.'

'Well, I can tell you absolutely, positively that Petie is not going to die on Saturday.'

'All right, then, can he come over and spend the day and night with me?' My mom was very particular about people not getting hurt in our yard. Like she would say, 'I hope those little kids are not going to get hurt riding their bikes in our driveway,' as if it would be perfectly all right if they were hurt just out of our drive, in the street somewhere.

'Yes, you may have him over.'

This made me feel a little better, but as soon

as my dad got home, he came in and talked to me for over an hour about self-control and not letting myself get worked up over foolish things. He seemed to think I enjoyed getting worked up and upset over my friend's death. I didn't want to worry about things. I wanted to be peaceful and calm like everyone else, only sometimes I couldn't.

Anyway, Petie came over on Saturday and we were careful all day. We didn't even go to bed until it was twelve o'clock. Then, before we got in bed, we went out into the hall, and in the dark we found the telephone and dialled the time to make sure. When the operator said, 'The time is twelve-o-two,' Petie started jumping up and down and saying, 'I'm spared, I'm spared.'

My dad said, 'Be quiet out there.'

We went in and lay down on the bed, and for about an hour all we said were things like, 'Whew!' and 'What a relief!' and 'I really, honestly thought

I was going to die, Tom, didn't you?'

I thought about that, and how now that I was controlling myself perfectly, now that there could not be one single complaint of any kind about my absolutely perfect control, there was no one around to see it.

Four
Stranger

After supper Aunt Millie said, 'Well, I imagine you would like to get unpacked. I never even thought about that until this minute. Come on.'

We went upstairs and Aunt Millie walked to a room down at the end of the hall and said, 'There! I thought you would like to stay in Bubba's old room because it is just like it was when he left. I keep saying that I'm going to clean out this room and throw away all the junk, but I never do.'

I went into the room slowly and put my suitcase down on the rug. I knew right away what kind of boy Bubba had been by looking at that room. There was not a person in the world who could have thought the room was mine. Just one glance at me and *anyone* would know that I had never shouldered the shotgun on the rack, that I had never stuffed the squirrel on the bookcase, that I had never collected all those different bird eggs and nests in the bookcase.

Aunt Millie was saying, 'I have been after Fred for weeks to hammer those screens in. I know how boys love to climb out their windows at night. Come here.'

I went over, and she pointed to the huge tree beside the window. 'Look, there. See those smooth spots on the branches? Just like steps?

Well, that's how often my boys came up and down that old tree – their feet wore down the bark. They wouldn't use the stairs for anything. And I said, "Fred, I am through worrying about boys falling out of trees. You hammer the screens into those upstairs windows." '

'I won't climb out,' I assured her.

'Oh, go along with you. I know boys.'

'No, I'm afraid of heights.'

'Don't tell *me*. You'll be out there first chance you get. I know! Only, like Fred says, if you want to climb out, there's not a screen in the world could stop you, so I guess it doesn't matter.' She crossed to the chest and pulled out two drawers. 'Now I cleared out these drawers for you. Put your things right in here.' She patted the bottom of the drawer so I wouldn't make any mistake.

'Now, I'll be downstairs if you want anything.'

'I won't.'

'Well, if you do, I'll be downstairs.'

She went out, and I opened my suitcase and put my clothes in the drawers, and then I opened the other drawers and looked at all the things in them. There were different kinds of rocks in shoeboxes, and bullets, and an old card box with coins in it, and a big stack of 4-H project books, and in the bottom drawer were some old hunting clothes and bathing suits with life-saving emblems on them.

I closed the drawers and sat down on the edge of the bed. I had not been able to eat any supper at all. Aunt Millie had been watching me the whole time and she had said over and over, 'Don't you like the supper?' Finally I had managed to hide some food in my pocket so she would think I had eaten something. Now I reached into my pocket and took out the crumpled-up sandwich and two broken peanut-butter crackers.

The only time I ever really enjoyed eating was one time over at Petie's house. Petie was a great eater, and he got an idea for a new food invention. It was called The Petie Burkis Special. He got his mom to make up some dough, and then on top of this dough, Petie cut up dozens of hot sausages and luncheon meats and different kinds of cheese and pickles. Then he rolled it up and baked it, and when it came out of the oven it looked like a great golden football.

Petie sliced it right down the middle with a big knife and pushed half over to me. Wonderful-smelling steam poured up into my face. We started eating and our mouths were on fire and cheese and sausage juice was dripping down our chins. Petie was just moaning with happiness and I ate until my stomach hurt. It was the only time in my life that my stomach had hurt from being too full.

I sat there holding the crumpled sandwich in my

hand. It was pimento-cheese, which Aunt Millie had made specially, since they were her boys' favourites. She told me that one time on a picnic Bubba and Fred Jr together had eaten twenty-three halves of her pimento-cheese sandwiches. When I heard that, I had tried harder than ever to get one down, but I just couldn't. The only thing in all the world I could have eaten right then was a Petie Burkis Special, and then only if Petie himself had come running in with it.

Five

The Black Fox

The first three days on the farm were the longest, slowest days of my life. It seemed to me in those days that nothing was moving at all, not air, not time. Even the bees, the biggest fattest bees that I had ever seen, just seemed to hang in the air. The problem, or one of them, was that I was not an enormously adaptable person and I did not fit into new situations well.

I did a lot of just standing around those first days. I would be standing in the kitchen and Aunt Millie would turn around, stirring something, and bump into me and say, 'Oh, my goodness! You gave me a scare. I didn't even hear you come in. When *did* you come in?'

'Just a minute ago.'

'Well, I didn't hear you. You are so *quiet*.'

Or Uncle Fred would come out of the barn wiping his hands on a rag and there I'd be, just standing, and he'd say, 'Well, boy, how's it going?'

'Fine, Uncle Fred.'

'Good! Good! Don't get in any mischief now.'

'I won't.'

I spent a lot of time at the pond and walking down the road and back. I spent about an hour one afternoon hitting the end of an old rope swing that was hanging from a tree in the front yard. I made my two models, and then I took some of the spare plastic strips and rigged up a harness, so that the horse was pulling the car, and Aunt Millie got very excited over this bit of real nothing and said it was the cleverest thing she had ever seen.

I wrote a long letter to Petie. I went down to the stream and made boats of twigs and leaves and watched them float out of sight. I looked through about a hundred farm magazines. I weeded Aunt Millie's flowers while she stood over me saying, 'Not that, not *that*, that's a zinnia. Get the chickweed – see? Right here.' And she would snatch it up for me. I had none of the difficult chores that I had expected because the farm was so well run that everything was already planned without me. In all my life I have never spent longer, more miserable days, and I had to keep saying, 'I'm fine, just fine,' because people were asking how I was all the time.

The one highlight of my day was to go down

to the mailbox for the mail. This was the only thing I did all day that was of any use. Then, too, the honking of the mail truck would give me the feeling that there was a letter of great importance waiting for me in the box. I could hardly hurry down the road fast enough. Anyone watching me from behind would probably have seen only a cloud of dust, my feet would pound so fast. So far, the only mail I had received was a postcard from my mom with a picture of the statue of Liberty on it telling me how excited and happy she was.

This Thursday morning when I went to the mailbox there was a letter to me from Petie Burkis and I was never so glad to see anything in my life. I ripped it open and completely destroyed the envelope I was in such a hurry. And I thought that when I was a hundred years old, sitting in a chair with a rug over my knees, and my mail was brought in on a silver tray, if there was a letter from Petie Burkis on that tray, I would snatch it up and rip it open just like this. I could hardly get it unfolded – Petie folds his letters up small – I was so excited.

Dear Tom,
    There is nothing much happening here. I went to the playground Saturday after you left, and you know that steep bank by the swings? Well, I fell all the way down that.
    Here's the story:

BOY FALLS DOWN BANK WHILE GIRL ONLOOKERS CHEER

Today Petie Burkis fell down the bank at Harley Playground. It is reported that some ill-mannered girls at the park for a picnic cheered and laughed at the sight of the young, demolished boy. The brave youngster left the park unaided.

Not much else happened. Do you get Chiller Theatre? There was a real good movie on Saturday night about mushroom men.

Write me a letter,

Petie Burkis

I went in and gave the rest of the mail to Aunt Millie who said, 'Well, let's see what the government's sending us today,' and then I got my box of stationery and went outside.

There was a very nice place over the hill by the creek. There were trees so big I couldn't get my arms around them, and soft grass and rocks to sit on. They were planning to let the cows into this field later on, and then it wouldn't be as nice, but now it was the best place on the farm.

Incidentally, anyone interested in butterflies would have gone crazy. There must have been a million in that one field. I had thought about there being a contest – a butterfly contest and hundreds of people would come from all over the country to catch butterflies. I had thought about it so much that I could almost see this real fat lady from Maine running all over the field with about a hundred butterfly nets and a fruit jar under her arm.

Anyway, I sat down and wrote Petie a letter.

Dear Petie,

I do not know whether we get Chiller Theatre or not. Since there is no TV set here, it is very difficult to know what we could get if we had one.

My farm chores are feeding the pigs, feeding the chickens, weeding the flowers, getting the mail, things like that. I have a lot of time to myself and I am planning a movie about a planet

that collides with Earth, and this planet
and Earth become fused together, and
the people of Earth are terrified of the
planet, because it is very weird-looking
and they have heard these terrible
moanlike cries coming from the depths
of it. That's all so far.

Write me a letter,
Tom

I had just finished writing this letter and was waiting
for a minute to see if I would think of anything to
add when I looked up and saw the black fox. I did
not believe it for a minute. It was like my eyes were
playing a trick or something, because I was just
sort of staring across this field, thinking about my
letter, and then in the distance, where the grass was
very green, I saw a fox leaping over the crest of the

field. The grass moved and the fox sprang towards the movement, and then, seeing that it was just the wind that had caused the grass to move, she ran straight for the grove of trees where I was sitting.

It was so great that I wanted it to start over again, like you can turn movie film back and see yourself repeat some fine thing you have done, and I wanted to see the fox leaping over the grass again. In all my life I have never been so excited.

I did not move at all, but I could hear the paper in my hand shaking, and my heart seemed to have moved up in my body and got stuck in my throat.

The fox came straight towards the grove of trees. She wasn't afraid, and I knew she had not seen me against the tree. I stayed absolutely still even though I felt like jumping up and screaming, 'Aunt Millie! Uncle Fred! Come see this. It's a fox, a *fox*!'

Her steps as she crossed the field were lighter and quicker than a cat's. As she came closer I could see that her black fur was tipped with white. It was as if it were midnight and the moon were shining on her fur, frosting it. The wind parted her fur as it changed directions. Suddenly she stopped. She was ten feet away now, and with the changing of the wind she got my scent. She looked right at me.

I did not move for a moment and neither did she. Her head was cocked to one side, her tail curled up, her front left foot raised. In all my life I never saw anything like that fox standing there with her pale green golden eyes on me and this great black fur being blown by the wind.

Suddenly her nose quivered. It was such a slight movement I almost didn't see it, and then her mouth opened and I could see the pink tip of her tongue. She turned. She still was not afraid, but with a bound that was lighter than the wind – it was as if she was being blown away over the field – she was gone.

Still I didn't move. I couldn't. I couldn't believe that I had really seen the fox.

I had seen foxes before in zoos, but I was always in such a great hurry to get on to the good stuff that I was saying stupid things like, 'I want to see the go-rillllllas,' and not once had I ever really looked at a fox. Still, I could never remember seeing a black fox, not even in a zoo.

Also, there was a great deal of difference between seeing an animal in the zoo in front of painted fake rocks and trees and seeing one natural and free in the woods. It was like seeing a kite on the floor and then, later, seeing one up in the sky where it was supposed to be, pulling at the wind.

I started to pick up my pencil and write as quickly as I could, 'P.S. Today I saw a black fox.' But I didn't. This was the most exciting thing that had happened to me, and 'P.S. Today I saw a black fox' made it nothing. 'So what else is happening?'

Petie Burkis would probably write back. I folded my letter, put it in an envelope, and sat there.

I thought about this old newspaper that my dad had had in his desk drawer for years. It was orange and the headline was just one word, very big, the letters about twelve inches high. WAR! And I mean it was awesome to see that word like that, because you knew it was a word that was going to change your whole life, the whole world even. And every time I would see that newspaper, even though I wasn't even born when it was printed, I couldn't say anything for a minute or two.

Well, this was the way I felt right then about the black fox. I thought about a newspaper with just one word for a headline, very big, very black letters, twelve inches high. FOX! And even that did not show how awesome it had really been to me.

Six

Hazeline

I did not mention to anyone that I had seen the black fox. For one thing I did not want to share it, and then, too, I had never heard that there was such an animal. I had the uneasy feeling that someone would say, 'A *black* fox? Boy, you've been dreaming. There's no such thing as a black fox!'

That night, though, after supper I went out on

to the porch where Hazeline was sitting waiting for her boyfriend, who was coming to take her for a ride. She was reading a bride magazine and she said to me, 'How do you like that dress?'

'It's all right.'

'It would look awful on me though,' she said. 'I am too fat for *everything*.'

'I think you're just right. I think people who like to eat are very lucky.' I never saw anyone who liked to eat as much as Hazeline, not even Petie Burkis. Every night at the supper table she would say, 'This is the *best* cabbage (or sweet corn or beans or beets or whatever we were having) I have ever eaten in my *whole* life.'

'Well, I wish I was like you,' she said, 'and could just pick at my food. You would think that there never was such a thing as a fat bride, because in all this magazine there are only the tiniest skinniest girls you ever saw.' She showed them to me.

'Hazeline?'

She was now angrily flipping through the pages of skinny brides, showing them to me one by one.

'What?'

'Do you have many wild animals around here?'

'Wild animals?' She paused to turn her mind from the brides. 'Law, no, this is practically like the city now. You don't have to worry about wild animals.'

'No deer or – foxes, anything like that?'

'Oh, sure, deer, foxes, squirrels, muskrat, the woods are full of *them*. Dad and the boys used to go hunting all the time. I remember they shot a possum one time and it was the ugliest thing you ever saw and it had these tiny baby possums in its pouch. They were so tiny that Daddy had one in a spoon to show me, in a *teaspoon*!' She shuddered and closed her magazine. 'I squealed – I just squealed! I thought that possum in that teaspoon was the awfullest thing I ever saw. And Fred Jr and Bubba used to tease me about that for years. We would be sitting at the table and all of a sudden Fred Jr would make the awfullest face and say, 'Mamma! Hazeline's eating with the *possum* spoon!' That was the only way anybody could ever stop my eating. The *possum* spoon!' She let her magazine drop to the floor beside her chair.

'Hazeline, do you see many . . . foxes in the woods?'

'Why? You want to go hunting?'

'No, no, I just wanted to see an animal or something. I don't want to go hunting ever.'

'Well, if you do want to go, you just tell Daddy, because he is never happier than when he's walking through the woods with his gun. He loves it. He could go hunting every day of his life.'

'Do people do any trapping or anything around here?'

'No.'

'Never?'

'There used to be good money in trapping, I

58

guess, but now they got fur farms and things. Nobody I know does any trapping, unless it's 'cause an animal gets to be a bother, like in the garden or with the chickens.'

'Then what do they do?'

'Well, you know that house right on the opposite side of the road where you turn in to our place?'

I said quickly, 'Yes.'

'Well, it hadn't been but about two weeks ago that something was stealing that man's chickens. Every night a chicken would be gone, and he knew it was a fox.'

'How did he know that?'

'These chickens were taken just before they roosted or real early in the morning, maybe. If a hen's taken from a high perch or something, then it's generally a coon or an owl. If there's some of the chicken left uneaten, then it's generally a weasel or a skunk. But if the chicken's just gone –

just carried off whole with maybe a feather or two left behind – then it's a fox.'

'Oh.'

'Usually a fox won't bother your chickens except when it's got a family of little foxes or something. Then it'll come right on in and take what it wants and not make a noise doing it.'

'What did the man do?'

'Mr Hunter tried going out with his gun but he couldn't get near that fox. Foxes are tricky – that's not something that's just in stories. They really *are* tricky. So Mr Hunter got real tired of the whole thing and he went down to the creek and he put a piece of raw chicken out in the middle of the stream on a little island that the fox couldn't reach.' She broke off. 'Well, at last here comes that boyfriend of mine.'

'Yes, but go on about the fox.'

'Wait a minute.' She waited till her boyfriend got out of the car and then she called, 'Well, you were so late getting here that I just went and got me a new boyfriend.'

She laughed and hooked her arm through mine.

'Well, then,' he said, 'I reckon I'd just be wasting my time around here.' And he turned around and pretended to head back to the car.

'Mikey Galter, you come right back here.'

He came back and sat on the porch railing, grinned, tugged at the hem of her skirt, and said, 'You look mighty good.'

I said, 'Go on about the fox, Hazeline.'

She laughed and said, 'Where was I? Almost losing my boyfriend put that fox right out of my head.'

'Mr Hunter put the raw chicken on the island so the fox couldn't reach it,' I prompted.

'Yeah, well, then he put some moss in the stream like a little stepping stone, see? Only underneath the moss was an open trap, and that very night the fox came by and he saw the raw chicken and he put his foot right on that moss and sprung the trap. Bingo!'

'Oh.'

'End of fox,' she said. 'That was about two weeks ago, and then he found the den and went and got a stick of dynamite and blew it up and that was the end of the baby foxes.'

'Oh.' It was one of those stories that you're sorry afterwards that you made somebody tell you.

Mikey said, 'My grandaddy was the one who could get foxes. He used to be able to squeak them up.'

'What are you talking about?' Hazeline asked.

'There was a place like a hollow, where there were wood mice, and my grandaddy would get down in there and hide and start squeaking. That man sounded more like a mouse than any mouse. He could get a fox in rifle range every time. They just couldn't resist his squeaking.'

Hazeline said, real delighted, 'I didn't know your grandaddy could do that.'

Mikey nodded. 'He was in the kitchen one time and he started squeaking, and my mom came in and said, real worried, "There's a mouse somewhere in this kitchen. I hear it!"'

'Your mamma?' Hazeline asked.

'She's scared of mice, I'm telling you.'

'Not *your* mamma?'

'Yes, *my* mamma.'

They got up an argument about whether his mother was really scared of mice or not, and I said, 'I thought foxes were very smart.'

'They're smart, all right,' Mikey said. 'I got the smartest dog in the world and he has yet to catch him a fox. They been fooling him for ten years.'

'Henry? Is that who you're calling the smartest dog in the world?' Hazeline said, and then they started arguing about whether Henry was smart or dumb.

'Are we going to sit here and fight all night, or are we going for a ride?' Mikey said finally.

'Let me get my sweater,' Hazeline said. She did and then they went down the steps, Hazeline saying, 'Next time I see your grandaddy in church I'm going to ask him if he'll squeak like a mouse for me.'

I sat there a minute and then Aunt Millie called, 'Tom, come in here a minute.'

I went in the hall and she was standing back by the bookcase. She said, 'Your mother told me how much you like to read and we have just bushels of books right here. You take whatever you want.'

She opened the little glass doors so I could see the books and they were all the kind I didn't like. The way I liked to get a book was this:

I would go over to Petie's and he would be sitting on the porch reading. He would be so interested in the book that he wouldn't even look up to see who I was.

'What are you reading, Petie?'

He would lift the book so I could see the title and it would be something like *Mystery of the Deep*.

'Can I read it when you're through?'

He would nod.

'How much more you got?'

Still without missing a word, he would flip the remaining pages.

'Well, hurry up, will you?'

He would nod again, but Petie Burkis had never hurried through a book in his life. So I would wait. And I would wait. And wait. And finally, when I was ready to go out and get the book out of the library myself, then he would come over and give it to me. I couldn't get it open fast enough and I would start reading on my way into the house and the book would start like, 'The crack in the earth appeared during the night and when the people of Pittsburgh awoke, it was there, and deep down in

65

the crack the people could see something moving.'

That was the way I liked to get a book. I did not like to open a bookcase, especially with someone watching, and know that I had to take one, *had* to.

'This one looks good,' I said. It was the kind of book I particularly hated. It was called *The Lamb Who Thought He Was a Cat*. I used to wish people wouldn't write books like that. It would make me feel sad to read about someone who was trying to be something he could never, ever be in his whole life. Just thinking about that lamb worrying because he couldn't climb trees or because he didn't have claws made me feel awful.

'That's a wonderful book,' Aunt Millie said. 'We laughed over that thing. I can still remember Bubba sitting in that chair right over there laughing at that book.' She looked pleased at my selection.

'I think I'll take it outside,' I said.

'Now, listen, when it starts getting dark, you

come in. I don't want you to ruin your eyes.'

Ruining my eyes was something she did not have to worry about, but adults always seemed to be worrying about the wrong things. One time Petie Burkis's sitter came out and Petie was stuck up in this tree, about to fall, and she said, 'Petie, come down out of that wind – you're going to get the earache!' Petie made up a headline about it – BOY BREAKS TWENTY-SEVEN BONES – AVOIDS EARACHE!

'Now, when it gets dark, come on in.'

'Sure.'

I went out and sat by the creek on the very rock I had sat on that morning. I did not open the book. I turned it front down on the grass beside me, because I did not even want to see the lamb and the cat on the cover. And I sat there looking across the field, waiting, hoping for some miracle that would bring the black fox leaping over the green, green grass again.

Seven

Discovery at the Field

The next four days I spent practically the whole time down by the creek waiting to see the black fox. I am not a good patient waiter. I like to have things go ahead and happen. I thought one time that if there was some way to turn your life ahead like a clock, then I would probably lose half my life turning it ahead to avoid waiting for things.

On Tuesday I was sitting there as usual, and I don't believe I ever saw anything as green as that field was that day. The sun had turned the grass a sort of golden-green. It was like looking at the grass through sunglasses.

And I thought that if I could discover one thing in my life, I would like to discover a fabulous new colour – a brand-new colour that no one had ever seen before. Here's how it would be.

I would be digging in my back yard and all of a sudden while I was just casually digging, I would get this strange exciting feeling that something exceptionally good was about to happen. I would begin to dig faster and faster, my heart pumping in my throat, my hands flashing in the soft black dirt. And suddenly I would stop and put my hands up to my eyes. Because there, in the black earth, would be a ball, a perfectly round mass of this brand-new colour.

I would not be able to take it in for a moment, because I wouldn't ever have seen anything but blue and green and all, but gradually my eyes would adjust and I would see – I would be the first person in all the world to see this new colour.

I would go into the house and say to my parents, 'I have discovered a new colour,' and my parents would not be particularly interested, because there *is* no such thing as a new colour, and they would be expecting me to bring out a piece of paper on which I had mixed a lot of different water colours and made just an odd colour, and then slowly I would take my hand from my pocket and hold up the smooth round ball of new colour.

That night I would be on the news with my discovery and the announcer would say, 'Ladies and Gentlemen, if you know someone who has a colour television, go there immediately, because tonight you will see, later in our programme, a new

70

colour, discovered today by a young boy.' And by the time I came on the television, every person in the world would be sitting in front of his set.

The announcer would say, 'Now, young man, would you tell the world how you came to discover this new colour.'

'I was outside digging in the dirt –'

'Where was this dirt?'

'Just in my back yard. And I got a strange feeling –'

'What was this strange feeling like?'

'It was the feeling that I was about to make a new and important discovery.'

'I see. Go on.'

'And I dug deeper and deeper, and then I looked down into the earth and I saw – *this!*' And I would bring forth the new colour, and all around the world a silence would occur. The only silence that had ever fallen upon the whole world at one time. Eskimoes would pause with pieces of dried fish halfway to their mouths; Russians who had run in from the cold would stop beating the snow from their arms; fishermen would leave their nets untended. And then, together, all at once, everyone in the world would say, '*Ahhhhhhhhhhh.*'

I was so interested in thinking about my discovery that I almost missed seeing the black fox.

There were some old tree stumps in the field that stuck up above the grass. Several times I thought one of these stumps had moved and that the black fox had come at last. I had kept quite still and waited until the stump became, again, a tree stump.

Now suddenly – I was looking in the right direction or I might have missed it – the black fox appeared on the crest of the hill. Gracefully, without hurrying, she moved towards me. There was no wind at all; the air was perfectly still; and

Hazeline had told me that on windless days foxes liked to hunt mice. The way they catch them is by watching for the faint movements of the grass. The mice run below the grass in little paths. The fox crouched low. She did not move. I could see her head above the grass, the sharp pointed ears. She waited, and then slowly, without seeming to move at all, she stretched up, rising tall in the grass. She paused.

Her eyes watched the grass. Suddenly she saw what she was looking for, and she pounced. It was a light, graceful movement, but there was power in her slim black legs, and when she brought her head up, she had a mouse between her jaws.

She turned, her full tail high in the air, and moved towards the woods. I stood up slowly and watched as she trotted away among the trees.

Eight

The Forest Chase

It was impulse more than anything else that made me follow the black fox, and the desire to see where she was going and what she was going to do. I walked quickly across the field to the woods.

I cannot exactly explain my fascination with this fox. It was as if I had just learned a new and exciting game that I wanted to play more than anything else in the world. It was like when Petie Burkis first learned to play Monopoly, and that was all he wanted to do – just play Monopoly. One time he followed me around the yard on his knees, begging me to play with him. And one time he made his sitter play with him and he did everything for her – collected her money, moved her piece, paid her rent. All she did was sit there reading a magazine.

That's the way I felt about this fox. It was a new game. The rules I didn't exactly know yet; all I had so far was a fierce desire to play. My father once said this could be the most important thing in any game.

I slipped through the trees, and the forest was warm and sunlit. All around were large wrinkled boulders. It was as if hundreds of full skirts had been left on the forest floor to dry. There was not a sound anywhere, and I had the feeling I was the only living being in the whole forest.

In English class one time we had to say poems and one girl recited this poem called 'Where Are All the Forest Folk?' And when she started speaking, big tears started rolling down her cheeks. There was no noise at first, just big tears dropping down on to her blouse, but when she got to the line 'The gay little chipmunk romps no more,' she really started sobbing. She could hardly go on she was crying so hard. The teacher said, 'Ruth Ann, maybe you'd rather finish later,' but Ruth Ann wouldn't sit down, and by the time she got to the last line, which was something like 'Oh, where are all the forest folk who were so dear to me?' every girl in the whole room was sobbing. Mrs Heydon said, 'Girls, girls!' and then, 'Is there anyone who has a gay poem?' Petie said he was ready with his original composition, entitled 'TV Land', but even that didn't help much. You would have thought that the saddest thing those girls would ever know in their lives would be an empty forest.

That, I thought that day, is exactly what I have come upon now. I walked slowly towards a thicket of pines to the right, and just then I heard crows beyond the trees. Hazeline had told me that crows were great thieves. She had once seen a bunch of crows make a fox drop a hen and run off, and I thought perhaps these crows had seen the black fox with her mouse. I charged through the pines and then, to the left, I heard the sharp bark of the fox.

I stood perfectly still, waiting. A butterfly lit on the stone by my foot and flexed its wings. The bark came again. A high, clear bark. I turned and began to run around the pine thicket towards a rocky ravine. The underbrush was thick here, and briars scratched my legs. I ran past the ravine and on through the trees. The fox barked again and I ran even faster.

I don't know how far I went, or in exactly which

direction, but I finally stopped by a huge old tree and sat down on a root. There was not a sound anywhere now. I waited. I had had the feeling, all the while I was running, that the black fox had been calling me, leading me somewhere, and now I had lost her.

I turned my head slowly, listening. I could not give up the idea that the fox had wanted me to follow her. I imagined all sorts of things as I got up and reluctantly began to walk back through the forest. The kind of thing I was imagining was that a giant boulder had accidentally rolled over the opening to the fox's den, trapping her family inside, and now the fox was leading me to the den, so that I could push the stone aside for her.

I paused from time to time and listened, but I heard nothing from the black fox. I continued to walk until I came out of the forest, right by the pasture where the cows were grazing. They were all together in the shade of the trees, and they turned in a body and looked at me.

I had thought, when I first saw these cows from a distance, that if I ever had to do a circus act, I would get about six cows like these and train them. They would be called The Cow Family Dancers, and I would come out in an Alpine suit with an accordion, and as I would start to play, the cows would come dancing out into the circus arena, not trotting like horses, but doing peasant steps, turning and clicking their heels and tossing their heads.

Now that I saw the cows at close range I abandoned this idea for all time and began to walk slowly past them. 'Cows do *not* attack people. Cows do not *attack* people. Cows do not attack *people*.' Then, completely against my will, I found myself making up a Petie Burkis news story:

COW ATTACKS BOY — SCIENTISTS BAFFLED

Scientists in Clinton County were baffled today by the report that a cow attacked a young boy. The young boy, who was passing the cow in a respectful manner, was able to give no reason for the attack. 'She just came at me,' he managed to whisper before he was driven away to the hospital. No one has been able to reach the parents of the young boy, as they are having a vacation in Europe.

At this point one of the cows actually did take a step in my direction and I began to run down the hill. I ran past the cows, crashed into the fence, got up and brushed myself off, crawled under the fence, and ran on into the yard.

'Well, what on earth's the matter with you?' Hazeline said. She was taking clothes off the line.

'I was just running.'

'Anything after you?'

'No.'

'I thought maybe you'd stirred up an old bear or something.'

'No.' I did not say that I was running from an interested cow, because even Hazeline might not be able to resist the temptation to make sport of that.

She went back to her clothes. I never saw anyone take clothes from a line so fast. With one hand she kept lifting off the clothes pins until she was holding about a hundred.

'Hazeline?'

'What?'

'I followed a fox in the woods.'

'Did you?' She deposited the clothes pins in an apron pocket.

'This fox acted like she wanted me to follow her.'

'You were probably near her den and she wanted

81

to lead you off. That is the oldest trick in the world. It'll fool a dog every time. But you – next time a fox tries to lead you off, you remember that if you keep looking around where you are, you just might see yourself some baby foxes.'

The idea was so appealing that I wanted to go back to the woods right away.

'It looked like it was a black fox.' I could no longer keep this information to myself.

'Oh.' She seemed more interested in the fact that she only had one blue sock left and no mate. This was why I could talk to her. Information just poured out of her and then she would forget it. She would never say at the supper table, the way some girls would, something like, 'Well, guess who thought he saw a black fox today?'

'Have you ever seen a black fox, Hazeline?'

'I saw one on a coat one time.' She found the blue sock and put all the clothes in the basket.

'The fur was about *that* thick. It looked so warm and soft. This lady in front of me in church had it on and I kept putting out my hands wanting to stroke it.'

'Is a black fox different from a red one?'

'I don't know. Listen, you ask Dad about foxes. When it comes to hunting animals there isn't anything he doesn't know.'

'I don't want to bother your dad.'

'Oh, he'd be real tickled. He loves to talk about the woods and all. Why, if you wanted him to find you a black fox, he could go out and do it.'

Nine

Uncle Fred

I still did not feel at ease with Uncle Fred. He was a large man, very powerfully built, and to see us together you would think we would make the perfect cover picture for a story called 'The Boy Who Tried To Be a Man'. There was a tremendous physical difference between us, and there was something else I don't know how to explain. We couldn't talk to each other. One time he took me to the lake and I couldn't think of one single thing to say all the way over or back. It was an awful feeling not to be able to think of one single thing worth saying.

Every night before supper Uncle Fred would take a swim in the pond. It was a ritual. He would come out on the porch in his bathing suit, put his towel on the back of a chair, pause for a moment on the steps, and then he would start running. He would run until he was at the very edge of the pond and then he would dive – it was more like a launch really – his body straight out, and he would go almost halfway across the pond before he hit the water. Then he would swim across, back, come up, and dry off.

This night when he came up on the porch Hazeline and I were sitting in the swing.

'You youngsters ought to take a dip. Makes you feel good.'

'The water's too warm,' Hazeline said. 'I can't stand to swim in warm water. It's real ucky.'

Uncle Fred was rubbing the towel over his head, so we couldn't hear exactly what he was saying, but it was something about Hazeline and me being a lot better off if we'd take a dip. This was my one big dread – that some night I would have to go swimming with Uncle Fred. I could imagine that while he was running and executing that long powerful dive, I would be wincing along (I had very sensitive feet) and then I would inch out into the water, terrified, and just stand there, bending my knees so everyone would think I was in deeper water than I was. Then, probably, to complete the horror, Uncle Fred would suggest that I climb up on his shoulders and dive off.

At that Hazeline would call from shore, 'Wait – let me get my camera. Wait now!' for she would consider it a wonderful thing to be able to snap a picture of a disaster. And she would run down and get us in focus – all the while I would be standing on Uncle Fred's shoulders, shaking – and then she would say, '*Go!*' With my whole body trembling I would fall forward into the muddy brown water, knowing that the last sight I would ever see would be the reflection of the sun on that muddy water.

They would ask my friend Petie Burkis to write a headline to go above the picture and he would write:

BOY DROWNS – GIRL PHOTOGRAPHS IT!

I went on thinking about that until Hazeline said, 'Dad?'

Uncle Fred draped his towel around his shoulders. 'What?'

'Tom and I were talking about foxes this afternoon –'

'Foxes?' he interrupted.

'Yes, and he was asking me about the different types of foxes, about black and red ones and all. And I told him you'd know.'

He rubbed the towel under his chin. 'Well, as far as I know – and I could be wrong about this – black foxes are sort of like an accident – like a black-haired baby born in a family of redheads. The pigment gets intensified and most of the time it'll be in just one fox in a litter. There'll be five cubs maybe and only one black one, and you can take two black foxes and mate them and get six red cubs.'

'Is a black fox smarter than a red one, do you think?' I asked.

'Supposed to be, has to be maybe, to keep out of the hunter's reach. A hunter'll do anything to get something rare.' He leaned back against the porch railing. 'When I was a boy – oh, this was a long time ago, but I still remember it – I saw a fight between a red fox and a black one. It was during the mating season, and it was over this little red fox who looked like she didn't give a darn for either one of them.'

'Playing it cool,' Hazeline said.

'I was up in a tree – I don't even remember what I was doing up there – probably some mischief – and in a little clearing ahead I saw these two foxes, one black with just a little white on him and the other red with a cross mark on his shoulders.'

I could almost see them. 'What was the fight like?'

'You ever see cats fight? Or dogs?'

I nodded my head.

'Well, that's the way this was. They were standing apart and walking around each other, just like dogs or cats, each testing the other, and all the time they were growling and snapping and darting at one another.' He moved his shoulders as if he were involved in the fight himself. 'Then the red fox sprang at the black one and just as quick as a whip that black fox brought his tail around – he had an enormous tail – and shielded his head with it. All the red fox got was a mouthful of fur.'

'What else?'

'Well, that was all I saw, because they moved on through the woods. The last I saw of them, this little lady fox was just the tiniest bit closer to the black fox than the red.'

'Sup-per!' Aunt Millie called.

'I better get myself dried off. You two go in.'

We went in and Aunt Millie said, 'Tom, there's a letter for you on the table in the hall.'

This letter from Petie Burkis had been there all day and I had not even seen it. I tore it open right there in the hall. It was so thick I thought Petie Burkis had written me about a ten-page letter and I wanted to see what he had to say. Instead, it was a questionnaire he had made up, and he said that if I would answer the questions and send it back to him he would be able to figure out what kind of person I was from my answers. He was so eager to have it returned that he had even included an envelope with his address on it. The questionnaire looked like this.

Circle the correct answer.

1. If you found a whole box of candy bars, would you
    (a) sell them
    (b) eat them
    (c) try to find the owner

2. How many TV commercials do you know by heart?
    (a) none

(b) more than none but less than five

(c) more than five

3. The kind of commercial you hate the most is

    (a) deodorant

    (b) mouthwash

4. The kind of hat you would most hate to wear is

    (a) a small man's hat with a feather

    (b) a checkered cap

    (c) a cap with a propeller on top

5. Which cereal would you buy?

    (a) Good Luckies – a cereal in the shape of horseshoes that is supposed to bring you good luck all day

    (b) Peppies – the cereal that cures that tired, run-down feeling

    (c) Friendlies – a cereal in the shape of

clasped hands that makes you have hundreds
of friends instantly

There were about fifty-two and they all sounded
like they were from a real test that you would take
in a magazine. Petie was good at this kind of thing.
He could imitate any sort of writing perfectly.

'My goodness, you certainly did get a nice long
letter from your friend,' Aunt Millie said. 'Come
on and get your supper and then you can read it.'

'All right.' Naturally I did not want to sit down
and eat supper when I had this whole questionnaire
to do, but I sat down anyway, kept the paper open
in my lap, and read while I was pretending to eat.

6. If you walked in your sleep, would you

      (a) say, 'Oh, well, lots of people walk in their
      sleep every night'

      (b) tie yourself to the bed

(c) invent a little camera and strap it to your
head so the next day you could develop the
film and see where you had been

'I said you could read the letter after supper,'
Aunt Millie said patiently. She always liked
everyone to give full attention to their eating.

'Oooo, this looks so good,' Hazeline said, happily
flapping open her napkin.

'Yes'm,' I said.

That night after I was in bed I lay awake for a
long time. I had a very good feeling. I had already
thought of a questionnaire I was going to make
up for Petie, and also I felt good because I had
seen the fox again.

Seeing something beautiful always made me feel
good. One time in a museum I saw an old model
of a sailing ship that someone had made long ago.
The sails were sewn just as carefully as sails that

really had to hold ocean winds, and the boards were fitted as well as boards that really had to keep water out, and I just stood there. I thought I would never get enough of looking at that old sailing ship.

My mom and dad practically had to pull me away, and even after we had left the museum and gone home, that was the only thing in the whole museum that I could remember.

My cousin Eleanor had gone with us to the museum and she had seen an old doll-house she liked, and as soon as we got home she started getting spools and boxes and stuff, and trying to make a doll-house just like the one she'd seen. But it was enough for me just to have seen that old ship and to know that it was there where I could see it again some time. Now, I felt the same way about the black fox.

Ten

The Search

The days and weeks passed quickly, long warm days in which I walked through the woods looking for the black fox.

The next time I saw her was in the late afternoon at the ravine.

This was my favourite place in the forest. The sides of the ravine were heavy dark boulders with mosses and ferns growing between the rocks, and at the bottom were trunks of old dead trees. The trunks were like statues in some old jungle temple, idols that had fallen and broken and would soon be lost in the creeping foliage. There was only an occasional patch of sunlight.

At the top of the ravine was a flat ledge that stuck out over the rocks, and I was lying there on my stomach this particular afternoon. The rock was warm because the sun had been on it since noon and I was half asleep when suddenly I saw something move below me. It was the black fox. There was a certain lightness, a quickness that I could not miss.

She came over the rocks as easily as a cat. Her tail was very high and full, like a sail that was bearing her forward. Her fur was black as coal, and when she was in the shadows all I could see was the white tip of her tail.

As I watched, she moved with great ease over one of the fallen trees, ran up the other side of the ravine, and disappeared into the underbrush.

I stayed exactly where I was. My head was resting on my arms, and everything was so still I could hear the ticking of my watch. I wanted to sit up. I am sort of a bony person and after I have been lying on something hard for a long time, I get very uncomfortable.

This afternoon, however, I did not move; I had the feeling that the fox was going to come back through the ravine and I did not want to miss seeing her.

While I was waiting I watched an ant run across the ledge with an insect wing. He was running so fast with this wing that he would make a little breeze and the wing would fly out of his grasp. Then he would go back and get the wing and start running again.

Then I watched some birds on the other side of the ravine circling over the rocks, catching insects as they skimmed the air. It was a beautiful sight, and I thought as I watched them, *that* is what man had in mind when he first said, 'I want to fly.' And I thought about some old genius working up in a remote mountain valley actually making a little flying machine that he could strap on his back like a knapsack, and this old man would come down to a big air base and he would go out on the flight line and announce to everyone, 'Folks, I have invented a flying machine.' There would be a silence and then everyone would start laughing as if they would never stop, and finally the Captain would pause long enough to explain to the old man that flying machines had *already* been invented, that right over there – that big silver thing with the huge wings, *that* was a flying machine, and over there, those enormous bullet-shaped things, *those* were flying machines. 'Well,' the old man would say, shaking his head sadly, 'I won't waste no more of your time. I'll just head on home,' and he would press a button on his knapsack, and silently, easy as a bird, he would lift off the ground, and skimming the air, fly towards the hills. For a moment everyone would be too stunned to move, and then the General would cry, 'Come back, come back,' and everyone at the air base would run beneath the flying old man, crying, 'Wait, wait, come back, come back!' because that was the way every one of those men really wanted to fly, free and easy and silent as a bird. But the old man, who was a little hard of hearing, would not hear their cries and would fly off into the distance and never be seen again.

Right after I stopped thinking about this, the black fox came back. She came down the rocks the same way she had gone up, her white-tipped tail as light as a plume, and I remembered a black knight I saw once in the movies who was so tall and fine and brave you could see his black plume racing ahead of all the other knights when there was a battle.

She had something in her mouth that looked like a frog – it probably was, for the creek was low now and you could always find a frog if you wanted one. She trotted on, apparently concerned only with getting the frog home, and yet I had the feeling that she was missing nothing. She passed across the ravine in a zigzag line and then started up the other side.

I did not move, and yet all at once she looked up at me. She froze for a moment, her bright eyes looking at me with curiosity rather than fear, and she cocked her head to one side, listening.

I stayed perfectly still – I was getting good at this – and we looked at each other. Then she turned away and bounded up the side of the ravine, turning at the top and disappearing into the underbrush. I felt that somewhere in the shelter of the trees she had paused to see if I was going to follow. Perhaps she wanted me to follow so she could lead me back into the forest, but I stayed where I was. After a while, I got up and went back to the farm.

The next time I saw the fox, it was a marvellous accident. These don't happen very often in real life, but they do happen, and that's what this was. Like the time Petie and I were walking down the alley behind his house and there, on top of this lady's garbage, we saw a mayonnaise jar full of marbles – not just ordinary marbles but all different kinds, kinds I had never seen before. Petie and I turned them all out on the grass and first Petie chose one and then I chose one until they were all gone. And both of us right now, today, have every single one of those marbles.

This was an even better accident. For the past two weeks I had been practically tearing the woods apart looking for the den of the black fox. I had poked under rocks and logs and stuck sticks in rotted trees, and it was a wonder that some animal had not come storming out and just bitten my hand off.

I had found a hornets' nest like a huge grey shield in a tree. I had found a bird's nest, low in a bush, with five pale-blue eggs and no mother to hatch them. I had found seven places where chipmunks lived. I had found a brown owl who never moved from one certain limb of one certain tree. I had heard a tree, split by lightning years ago, suddenly topple and crash to the ground, and I ran and got there in time to see a disgruntled possum run down the broken tree and into the woods. But I did not find the place where the black fox lived.

Now, on this day, I did not go into the woods at

all. I had gone up the creek where there was an old chimney, all that was left of somebody's cabin. I had asked Aunt Millie about it, but all she could remember was that some people named Bowden had worked on the farm a long time ago and had lived here. I poked around the old chimney for a while because I was hoping I would find something that had belonged to the Bowdens, and then I gave that up and walked around the bend.

I sat on a rock, perfectly still, for a long time and looked down into the creek. There were crayfish in the water – I could see them, sometimes partly hidden beneath a covering of sand, or I could see the tips of their claws at the edge of a rock. There were fish in the water so small I could almost see through them. They stayed right together, these fish, and they moved together too.

After a while I looked across the creek and I saw a hollow where there was a small clearing. There was an outcropping of rocks behind the clearing and an old log slanted against the rocks. Soft grass sloped down to the creek bank.

I don't know how long I sat there – I usually forgot about my watch when I was in the woods – but it was a long time. I was just sitting, not expecting anything or waiting for anything. And the black fox came through the bushes.

She set a bird she was carrying on the ground and beneath the rocks came a baby fox.

He did not look like his mother at all. He was tiny and woolly and he had a stubby nose. He stumbled out of the hole and fell on the bird as if he had not eaten in a month. I have never seen a fiercer fight in my life than the one that baby fox gave that dead bird. He shook it, pulled it, dragged it this way and that, all the while growling and looking about to see if anyone or anything was after his prize.

The black fox sat watching with an expression of great satisfaction. Mothers in a park sometimes watch their young children with this same fond, pleased expression. Her eyes were golden and very bright as she watched the tiny fox fall over the bird, rise, and shake it.

In his frenzy he dropped the bird, picked up an older dried bird wing in its place, and ran around the clearing. Then, realising his mistake, he returned and began to shake the bird with even greater fierceness. After a bit he made another mistake, dropping the bird by his mother's tail, and then trying to run off with that.

In the midst of all this, there was a noise. It was on the other side of the clearing, but the black fox froze. She made a faint sound, and at once the baby fox, still carrying his bird, disappeared into the den.

The black fox moved back into the underbrush

and waited. I could not see her but I knew she was waiting to lead the danger, if there was any, away from her baby. After a while I heard her bark from the woods, and I got up quietly and moved back down the creek. I did not want the black fox to see me and know that I had discovered her den. Hazeline had told me that foxes will pick up their young like cats and take them away if they think someone has discovered their den.

I wondered if this was how the black fox had come to have only one baby. Perhaps her den had been the one discovered by Mr Hunter. Perhaps she had started to move her cubs and had got only one to safety before Mr Hunter had arrived with his dynamite.

I decided I would never come back here to bother her. I knew I would be tempted, because already I wanted to see that fox play with his bird some more, but I would not do it. If I was to see the black fox again, it would be in the woods, or in the pasture, or in the ravine, but I was not going to come to the den ever again. I did not know that an awful thing was going to happen which would cause me to break this resolution.

I went home and I put a tiny little mark on the edge of my suitcase with my penknife. I did this every time I saw the black fox. There were four marks on my suitcase now, and in the weeks to come, there were to be ten more. Fourteen times I saw the black fox and most of those fourteen she saw me too. I think she knew that I wasn't anything to be afraid of. She didn't exactly jump with joy when she saw me and she didn't trust me, but I know she was not afraid.

After I got home, my mom said, 'What on earth happened to your brand-new suitcase? There are notches all over it.'

And I said, 'Let me see,' as if I was surprised

too, but if I wanted to, I could have sat right down then and told her about every one of those notches, that this one was for when I saw the black fox carrying home a live mouse so her baby could start learning to hunt for himself, and that this one was for when I saw the fox walking down the stream, her black legs shining like silk, and this one was for when the fox passed me so closely that I could have put out my hand and touched her thick soft fur. The fifteenth notch I never put in the suitcase, for that was not a happy memory like the others but a painful one.

Eleven
Tragedy Begins

One time Petie Burkis and I made up a TV show called 'This is your Bad Moment'. And on this show contestants would come out on the stage, and the audience would get to see the contestant in a bad moment. Like if Petie Burkis was a contestant he would come out on the stage and there would be an enormous table absolutely covered with every kind of pizza in the world. Petie loved pizza and he would just stand there looking at this steaming table and while he was deciding what kind of pizza to go for first, a little door would open and a hundred monkeys would come tumbling out, jump up on the table, and start romping all over the pizzas. Petie would leap forward, trying to save at least one, but he would be too late, and then the announcer's voice would say, 'Petie Burkis, this is your bad moment.' And the camera would come in close so everyone could see the sorrowful look on Petie's face as he watched the monkeys stomping on the pizzas.

Well, that night when Hazeline came out on the porch where I was sitting and said, 'Get on your bathing suit and let's take a swim,' I thought about that TV show. I could even hear the announcer's deep voice saying, 'Tommy, this is your bad moment.'

'What?' I said quickly.

'I said, let's take a swim. Didn't you bring your bathing suit?'

'I don't know.'

'Well, get on some old shorts then. Aren't you roasting?'

'I'm not so awfully hot.'

'Oh, come on.'

She got up and I followed her into the house and put on my bathing suit. I did not want to go swimming at all, but I went down and sat on the steps.

'Well, let's go,' Hazeline called from the corner of the house.

I looked up and she was standing there with two black inner tubes. In all my life I never saw a more welcome sight.

We went down to the pond and got in the inner tubes and just floated around. Hazeline kept saying, 'Don't splash me now. Don't splash,' until finally I got brave and did splash her a little, and then we just floated around some more.

I could have stayed in that inner tube for hours. I could have gone to sleep in that inner tube. It started getting dark and the stars came out, and I felt like that inner tube with me in it was the centre of the whole universe. I thought that if someone on another planet was looking at Earth through a tremendously powerful telescope, the first thing this person would see would be me and that black inner tube floating in the pond.

'There's Mikey,' Hazeline screamed suddenly. She always seemed surprised to see him, even though he had come over every single night since I had arrived. 'I've got on the awfullest bathing suit. Come on, let's get out and go around back before he sees us.'

We got out as quickly as we could, but of course

he saw us and came running over. He grabbed Hazeline by the arms and made her walk out on this little dock and then he pretended he was going to push her into the water.

'Mikey, really, Mikey, don't push me off, *really*, because I just washed my hair and this water is muddy. Mikey, I mean it, don't push me off, hear?'

He said, 'I'm not going to push you.'

'You are, too.'

'I am not going to push you.'

'Promise?'

'I promise. I am not going to *push* you. What I'm going to do is *drop* you.' And he held her out over the water and dropped her in.

She came up and she was furious. Her hair was like a sagging bird's nest, and she started thrashing her arms around and trying to splash Mikey. He ran out of the way, but Hazeline got a bucket and filled it with muddy water and she chased Mikey until she had him pinned against the hedge and then she said, 'All right, Mikey Galter, you just apologise to me or I'm going to throw this water all over you and your good shirt.'

He said, 'I'm sorry, I'm sorry, I'm sorry, I'm sorry –' And right then she threw the water all over him anyway and started running. It was very funny to watch and Aunt Millie and Uncle Fred came out and Uncle Fred said, 'Don't let her get away with that, Mikey,' and we were all laughing as if we would never stop.

Finally when it was over and they were drying off, I went up to my room and I felt the best I ever felt in my life. If someone had come up to me then with a paper and pencil and said, 'You may change one thing in this world. What will it be?' I would have said without hesitation, 'Nothing.'

I got in bed and lay there and I realised after a

while that there was a big smile on my face. For no reason I was lying there smiling. And then I turned over and went to sleep.

Petie Burkis had a sitter who could always tell when something bad was happening. One night she was sitting for Petie and she suddenly stood up and said, 'Someone in my family is in great danger.' Petie could see that she was really worried, so he told her it would be perfectly all right for her to call some of her relatives and warn them.

Well, she called everyone she could think of, even a half-sister in Virginia, and they were all fine. They all promised not to take any chances whatsoever for the next twenty-four hours, but the sitter still worried. She kept walking up and down the living-room saying, 'Someone I love is in danger, *grave* danger.' Petie said her hands were clasped together so tightly that her fingers were absolutely white.

When she got home that night – she called Petie the next day to tell him because he had been so nice – she found her cat lying on the doorstep half dead from a terrible fight, and she figured out that the cat had been in the fight at the very moment she had felt the danger. That cat, she told Petie, was just like a member of the family, because he had been with her for fourteen years.

I was just the opposite. I never suspected when something terrible was happening. For it was this very night, while I was lying there sleeping with a big smile on my face, that the tragedy of the black fox began.

Twelve

One Fear

Two days went by before I actually learned what had happened that night, because it was at supper on Friday that Aunt Millie said, 'A fox got my turkey that was nesting by the Christmas trees.'

My fork went down on my plate with a clang. I had been eating along just fine for weeks now, but after she said that I could not have swallowed if my

118

life had depended on it. It was like my food passage had suddenly shrunk to the size of a rubber band.

'No,' I protested.

Aunt Millie mistook my 'No' for a cry of outrage that some animal had dared to take her turkey.

She looked at me and nodded. 'I think it got one of the hens sometime last week too.'

Uncle Fred turned his iced-tea glass up and drained the contents.

'Well?' Aunt Millie said to him. She had been very irritable with all of us for a week. The heat was unbearable and with each passing day, as the ground got drier and the sun hotter, she had grown more fussy. She had been saying for days, 'I don't know what I'll do if it doesn't rain,' and now it was as if she had made up her mind, and what she had decided to do was take out all her ill feelings on my fox.

'I'm not going to put up with it,' she continued. 'I mean it, Fred. Once a fox gets started, he'll

119

clean out the whole henhouse. I have worked too hard on those hens to just stand by and watch some fox walk off with them one by one.'

'I know that, Millie.'

'Well, you are certainly acting mighty unconcerned about the whole thing,' she snapped. She pressed her napkin to her face. 'If the fox had made off with one of your precious pigs, I'd like to see what you'd do.'

'I'll take care of it,' Uncle Fred said.

'How?'

'After supper we'll go out and have a look,' he said with great patience.

I sat silent, trying to think of a plan, anything to divert them from the missing turkey. Finally I said, 'Maybe it wasn't a fox,' but Aunt Millie was already on her feet by that time saying, 'Well, let's go.'

'Now don't get in such an uproar.'

'I am not in an uproar, I am just concerned

about my chickens.'

'The heat's just got you down,' Uncle Fred said.

'It is *not* the heat. Every summer you start harping on the heat.'

'All right, it is not the heat,' Uncle Fred said. 'Let's go.' She left the dishes on the table, a thing I had never seen her do before, and the three of us walked out the back door. There was not a breeze anywhere in the yard and the leaves just hung on the trees. I had been so happy that this was the first time I had noticed how hot it really was. I felt as if my lungs were not going to be able to get enough oxygen out of this thick, hot air to keep me going.

'Turkey gone, eggs gone, cleaned out,' Aunt Millie said as we walked past the tree where the dog was tied. 'And you!' Aunt Millie pointed to the dog, who looked eagerly at us. 'You never even barked. Some watchdog you are.'

'Come on, Happ,' Uncle Fred said. He

unhooked the dog, who ran ahead of us as if to make up for his laxity.

We walked down the hill to where Uncle Fred had planted some trees to be cut for Christmas trees in a few years. Now they were no more than waist-high. 'This way,' Aunt Millie said, wading through the trees as if through a choppy sea. There were some bushes to the left and we followed her to them. She parted the bushes and we looked in silence at the empty nest. Only a few black feathers remained on the ground and one inside the nest, making it seem even emptier somehow.

With one hand Aunt Millie pointed towards the orchard, then slowly to the bushes, and then to the nest, as if tracing the path of the fox. And I, as she pointed, could imagine for myself exactly how it had happened.

The black fox had come gliding like a cat through the orchard, a small dark noiseless shadow moving between the trees. She had paused in the bushes, probably right where we were standing, looked through the leaves, and seen the turkey on its nest. She had remained there a moment, still as a statue, watching the turkey, which slept with its head under its wing.

The black fox had watched a moment more – she was not an impetuous hunter – and then, suddenly, without a sound, she had leaped to the nest. There was a silent struggle. Black wings beat the air and then drooped, and the struggle was over.

'He took the turkey,' Aunt Millie said, 'and never even cracked an egg doing it.' The ease of the thing seemed to make it even worse.

The dog was sniffing the ground and running first in one direction, then in the other.

'I don't see any eggs though,' I said.

'Sure you don't,' Aunt Millie said. 'Fox took them too.'

'Would a fox take eggs, Uncle Fred?'

He nodded. 'He'll take eggs and hide them till he wants them.'

'Where would he hide them?'

'Want to go look?' Uncle Fred said. 'Come on.'

'Well, if you two are going on an Easter-egg hunt, I'm going back and do the dishes.' She looked displeased. 'I don't know what good it'll do you to find the eggs now.' She turned and went through the little Christmas trees without looking back.

'Come on,' Uncle Fred said.

Without a word we skirted the Christmas trees and walked through the orchard.

One time my mom and dad had me sit down and make a list of all the things I was afraid of, because they thought that if I wrote all these fears down on paper – things like being afraid of high places and being afraid of dogs – I would see how foolish my fears were.

Well, I wrote them all down and it took me two notebook pages, back and front, and I took it in and showed it to my mom and dad and they looked very surprised, because even they had not expected four whole pages of fears. I think, in all, there was a total of thirty-eight different fears. At the moment, I thought that all those thirty-eight different fears put together were not as bad as this one fear I had right now – that something terrible was going to happen to the black fox.

We crossed a field where the trees had been cut and lay across the grass waiting to be sawed and moved. Then we came to the stream and paused. Still neither of us spoke.

Slowly Uncle Fred began walking up the stream. He was so interested now that he didn't even seem to notice when his foot slipped into the water and got wet. He paused several times, then continued until we came to a place where there was a sand bar under a high bank. He looked for a moment, and then with a smile he bent down and began to scoop aside the sand with his hand.

When the hole was about six inches deep he said, 'There!' He held up a turkey egg, a large tan egg with brown speckles, and then he stepped aside and I looked down into the hole and saw two more eggs in the sand.

'That's winter storage,' he said. 'Some old fox is planning to come back here when food's scarce and have an egg dinner.'

He put the turkey egg in my hand, and it was cold and damp. Then he said, 'It looks like you and I are going to have to do something about that fox.'

I had known all along that this was what it would come to. From the moment Aunt Millie had said a fox had gotten her turkey, I had known this would happen. Still, just the way Uncle Fred said it made me feel sick all over.

'Uncle Fred?' My mouth took this opportunity to make a five-syllable word out of his name. I thought he would look at me to see what was wrong, but he did not.

'What?' With the toe of his wet shoe he pushed the sand back into the hole.

'Maybe the fox is a hundred miles away by now.'

He shrugged. 'Tomorrow afternoon we'll go see,' he said. 'We'll take Happ and go into the woods.' He clapped me on the back with his hand – it was the first time he had ever touched me – and I could see that he was excited about going after the fox.

The turkey egg dropped from my hand, cracked on a rock, and the yolk began to stain the water.

'Let's go,' he said.

We stepped up the bank and across the fallen trees. And as we came to the orchard, my nose started to run.

Thirteen

Tacooma!

Suddenly, as we walked, I started thinking of this one word – *Tacooma*. The past summer I had gone to a very crummy Indian camp in the mountains. I only stayed five days because I got sick, but I remember this word *Tacooma* very well. The counsellors had told us the first night we were there, having something called the Opening Powwow, that *Tacooma* was an Indian word that meant 'Help me, Brother,' and they told us that it was a rule – an iron, never-to-be-broken rule – that if anyone ever came up to you, clasped your wrist 'where the blood flows', and said 'Tacooma!' you would have to help him. No matter what he wanted, you would *have* to help him. Otherwise, the old Indian legend said, the blood in your wrist would flow no more.

All the while I was at camp this worried me, because I was always afraid that someone was going to come up to me and say 'Tacooma' and I would have to do something awful like rush into the lake and pull his drowning friend from the deep, dark water by the rocks where we were not allowed to swim because of the snakes. Or at night, someone would awaken me in my bunk, clasp my wrist, say the dreaded 'Tacooma' and I would have to get up and walk down the black slippery path with him to the toilets. In my nightmares I heard the word *Tacooma* again and again.

Tonight, though, I thought that there should be a worldwide word like *Tacooma*, and you could use this word maybe three times in your whole life, and when you did use it, even a perfect stranger would have to help you, because even a perfect stranger would know that you would never, ever use one of your *Tacooma*'s unless it was a matter of vital importance. I thought how nice it would be right now if I could turn to Uncle Fred, clasp my hand around his thick hairy wrist, feel the blood pounding there, and say, 'Uncle Fred?'

Something in my voice would cause him to stop and look down at me.

'Uncle Fred, don't harm that fox.'

He would sputter, 'But that fox is making off with Millie's birds. You saw how upset she was at supper. She –'

'Uncle Fred,' I would interrupt. 'Tacooma!'

He would pause and then say in the quietest voice, 'The fox is safe. She will never be harmed here. I will explain to Millie.'

'Thank you, Uncle Fred.'

This was what I thought about all the way back to the farm. It was an awful feeling to want to help someone as badly as I wanted to help that black fox. My one hope – I decided this as we came to the house – was Hazeline.

She had gone out to the lake with Mikey on a picnic and would not be back till late, so I waited out on the porch for a while and then I went up in my room and sat in a chair by the window. All the time I was watching for the car headlights to come up the road, I was thinking about the fox. The dog was still running and I could hear his measured barks in the woods and once I thought I heard a high yapping sound like the bark of the fox.

It was almost midnight when I saw the car

lights. The car stopped and Hazeline got out and ran into the house. Usually she and Mikey stayed in the car a few minutes laughing and talking, so I was glad to see that tonight there weren't going to be any such delays.

She came up the steps very quickly, went into her room, and shut the door. I went across the hall and knocked.

'I'm getting ready for bed,' she said.

'Can I see you for just a minute, Hazeline?' I asked.

'What for?'

'I want to talk to you.'

There was a silence. I waited, then said, 'I *have* to talk to you.'

'Oh, come on in.'

I went in and she was lying across the bed with her face turned away. She had not started getting ready for bed at all but was still in the plaid playsuit she had worn to the picnic.

'Hazeline,' I began.

She turned around and I saw that her eyes were all red and swollen. She must have been crying for hours to get her face in such an awful condition. You could hardly even see where her eyes were.

'What's wrong, Hazeline?' I thought that if she had been soaking her whole head in hot water for four hours it wouldn't look this bad. She looked like Uncle Fred's prize pig, Rowina. 'What's wrong?'

'I'm not getting married – that's what's wrong,' she said.

'You mean you're not going to marry Mikey?'

'I mean Mikey's not going to marry *me*.' And she started to cry again.

I wanted to turn around and get out of that room as fast as I could. Only the fact that I desperately needed help for the black fox and that I thought Hazeline might know what to do kept me there. 'He'll marry you, Hazeline,' I said. I hoped Mikey had not been able to see how awful she looked with her face all swollen or he probably *wouldn't* marry her.

'No, he won't either.'

'Then you can marry someone else,' I said.

She looked up at me and stopped crying long enough to say, 'Who?' Then she waited.

'I don't know exactly who, but I know you'll get married.'

'I won't get married. I'm too *fat*!' She began to cry again. You could hardly believe that there were any tears left. I got a new respect for the tear glands then and there, because I saw that those glands could really manufacture tears when they had to. I wished that Petie were there to make up a headline. All I could think of was FARM GIRL'S EYES PRODUCE RECORD-BREAKING EIGHT HOURS OF TEARS – YOUNG FRIEND STANDS BY HELPLESSLY, which was too long.

'I don't think you're too fat,' I said finally.

'Well, Mikey thinks so. He says he's not going to marry me unless I lose twenty pounds.'

'Then just lose the twenty pounds, Hazeline. That's all you have to do and he'll marry you.'

'I can't. I just can't. I'm never going to get married. I'm going to be like old Miss Helva.'

'Who?'

'That fat old lady that was over last week, and all she comes over for is to eat. That's all. Eat, eat, eat! That's how I'm going to be. I'll be going around to people's houses hoping they've just made a cake or a pie – one time right down there in our kitchen I saw Miss Helva eat a whole berry pie!'

'Hazeline, you won't be like that. It's silly to even think so. Now, listen a minute,' I said, because it seemed to me she was quieting down. 'I need some help.'

'*You* need help!' She put her head down on her arm.

'Hazeline, you know that fox I've been talking about? The black fox?'

'Oh, I don't want to hear about foxes. I just want to marry Mikey and I can't lose twenty pounds. I can't.'

'Hazeline, your father is going to kill that fox.' This was the first time I had let myself actually think these words, much less say them, and I suddenly started shaking.

She turned around and looked at me, and I thought at last I had gotten through to her and she understood. I leaned forward and she said, 'Look, will you go downstairs and get me a banana?'

'What?'

'A banana. Maybe if I eat something I'll feel a little better. I couldn't hardly eat anything at the picnic I was so upset, and now I feel awful. My legs are real weak.' I hurried down to get the banana, and Aunt Millie met me in the hall, her cotton bathrobe held in front of her. 'Are you all right?' she asked. She always did this. Hazeline had been crying very loudly for a half-hour and she hadn't even heard that, but every time I so much as tiptoed to the bathroom for a drink of water she would come out of her room and say, 'Are you all right?'

'I'm just getting a banana for Hazeline.'

'Well, you need your rest. Don't you be running errands for her all night.'

'Peel it and put some peanut butter on it,' Hazeline called down the stairs.

I took the peeled and peanut-buttered banana up to Hazeline and waited till she ate it. I would have brought her a dozen bananas if I'd thought it would raise her spirits enough to help me. When she had finished, I said again, 'Hazeline, I need your help.'

'Listen, I can't do anything about your fox! I can't do anything about *anything*. I just feel terrible. You don't know what it's like to lose everything you want in one night.'

I went out and shut the door and walked across the hall to my room. I saw this movie on TV one time about a king who suddenly found out that in all his castle there was not one man, not *one*, who would help him fight the Red King of Crete. This king stood on his balcony, all alone, looking over his kingdom, which would soon be lost, and his face had a terrible lonely look. That was how I felt as I stood at the window looking out over the ragged line of the forest. I felt so much like that king that I thought if I put my hand up to my face, my face would feel very old and wrinkled and lonely.

I heard the sound of the hound in the woods again, and I knew that the black fox was out there now running beneath the trees. To me she was worth a hundred turkeys and hens. I wished suddenly that

I had lots of money and could go down to Aunt Millie and say, 'Here! I want to buy every hen and turkey you have on behalf of the black fox. They are all to belong to her, and she may come and get them whenever she chooses.' And Aunt Millie would tuck the money in her apron pocket and say, 'The turkeys and hens are now the property of the black fox.'

I walked over and sat on my bed and I suddenly felt worse than ever, because I remembered how that king had saved his castle from the Red King of Crete. He sent his daughter to get Hercules, who was waiting in the nearby hills, and Hercules, shining with sweat and muscles, arrived just in time to do battle and send the entire Cretan army limping back to their ships. Then the king had only to reward Hercules with the gift of his beautiful daughter, and the story came to a satisfying end while the people of the kingdom danced and sang for joy. So I was not like the lonely king after all. I had no beautiful daughter, no muscular friend waiting in the hills, and I knew that my story would not end with wild song and joyous dancing, but with a runny nose and wet eyes.

Fourteen

Unwilling Hunter

The next morning was hot and dry, and when I looked out of my window the air was brown with dust. I could hardly see the forest. It was like the dust had become magnetised by the sun and was rising to meet it.

Happ was lying in the yard under a tree. He had given up his chase at some point during the night and was now in a state of collapse. The heat was already unbearable. The earth had not cooled off during the night and now the sun had already begun to reheat it.

I went downstairs and the only person at the table with any animation was Uncle Fred. Hazeline was sitting with her chin in her hand, sullenly dipping a slice of toast into her coffee and then nibbling at it. Aunt Millie usually sat straight as a broom, but this morning she too was leaning forward on the table. 'Sit down and get yourself some cereal.'

I sat down and she said, 'I swear if we don't get some rain we are all going to dry up and blow away like the crops.'

'I'm going to start pumping water from the pond this morning,' Uncle Fred said.

'It won't do any good.' Aunt Millie turned her napkin over in her lap as if she were looking for the cool side.

'And then this afternoon,' Uncle Fred said to me, 'you and I'll go after the fox.' I could see that it was this thought that had caused his spirits to rise. 'Right?'

'Yes.' I did not want to go, of course, but I had the idea that if I was there, if I was right at his elbow every minute, there might come a time when I could jar his elbow as he fired his gun and save the fox. It was a noble thought but I knew even then it wasn't going to work.

'In case anyone is interested,' Hazeline said in a low voice, 'Mikey is not going to marry me.'

'What, Hazeline?'

'I said *Mikey's not going to marry me*!' And she slammed down her napkin and left the room.

'What is *that* all about?' Uncle Fred asked.

'Mikey's not going to marry her unless she loses twenty pounds,' I said.

'I cannot stand one more thing. I cannot!' Aunt

Millie said. 'If one more thing happens in this house I just don't know what I'm going to do.'

'Now, now. Mikey is going to marry Hazeline. The rain is going to come. And we are going to get the fox that's after your chickens,' Uncle Fred said. 'Come on, Tom, help me with the pump.'

'Well, don't let the boy get a heatstroke out there,' Aunt Millie said. 'I mean it. That will be absolutely the last straw.'

'I'll be all right.'

It was afternoon before the pump was working and the muddy water was moving between the small, dusty rows of vegetables.

'Well, that's that. Now, let's take some time off and go into the woods.' Uncle Fred paused, then said, 'If you're too tired, you don't have to come.'

'No, I want to.'

He looked pleased. 'I think you'll enjoy it.'

We went to the house and I waited on the back

steps while Uncle Fred went in and got his gun. He came out carrying it, muzzle down, and I could tell just from the way he held it that he knew everything there was to know about that particular gun. I knew that his hands had been over that gun so many times that, blindfolded, he could load it and aim it and probably hit whatever he wanted.

'Let's go.'

It was like in an army movie when the sergeant says, 'All right, men, let's move out,' and all the tired discouraged soldiers get up, dust themselves off, and start walking. I fell behind Uncle Fred and we went through the orchard – Happ leading the way – and down to the creek. We passed the place where we had found the turkey eggs, passed the place where I had sat and first seen the black fox. There! My eyes found the very spot where I had first seen her coming over the crest of the hill.

Uncle Fred crossed the creek in one leap – the

water was that low now – and stepped up the bank. Silently I followed. 'Fox tracks,' he said, and with the muzzle of his gun he pointed down to the tiny imprints in the sand. I had not even noticed them.

If I had hoped that Uncle Fred was not going to be able to find the black fox, I now gave up this hope once and for all. What it had taken me weeks and a lucky accident to accomplish, he would do in a few hours.

'The fox must be up there in the woods,' I said eagerly, knowing she was not, or that if she was, she had gone there only to make a false track.

'Maybe,' Uncle Fred said.

'Let's go there then,' I said and I sounded like a quarrelsome, impatient child.

'Don't be in too big a hurry. Let's look a bit.'

Happ had caught the scent of something and he ran up the creek bank, circled the field, then returned. Uncle Fred walked slowly along the bank. We were now about half a mile from the fox's den. If we kept on walking up the creek, past the fallen tree, past the old chimney, if we rounded a bend and looked up through the brambles in a certain way, then we could see the fox's den. It seemed to me as I stood there, sick with the heat and with dread, that the fox's den was the plainest thing in the world. As soon as we rounded the bend, Uncle Fred would exclaim, 'There it is.'

I said again, 'Why don't we go up in the woods and look? I think the fox's up there.'

'I'm not looking for the fox,' he said. 'We could chase that fox all day and never get her. I'm looking for the den.' He walked a few feet further and then paused. He knelt and held up a white feather. 'One of Millie's chickens,' he said. 'Hasn't been enough breeze in a week to blow it six inches. Come on.'

We walked on along the creek bank in the

direction I had feared. I was now overtaken by a feeling of utter hopelessness. My shoulders felt very heavy and I thought I was going to be sick. Usually when something terrible happened, I would get sick, but this time I kept plodding along right behind Uncle Fred. I could not get it out of my mind that the fox's life might depend on me. I stumbled over a root, went down on my knees, and scrambled to my feet. Uncle Fred looked back long enough to see that I was still behind him and then continued slowly, cautiously watching the ground, the woods, everything. Nothing could escape those sharp eyes.

Suddenly we heard, from the woods above, the short high bark I knew so well. The black fox! Uncle Fred lifted his head and at once Happ left the creek bank and dashed away into the woods. He bayed as he caught the scent of the fox, and then his voice, like the sound of a foghorn, was lost in the distant trees.

'That was the fox,' I said.

Uncle Fred nodded. Slowly he continued to move up the creek, stepping over logs, rocks, brushing aside weeds, his eyes and the muzzle of his gun turned always to the ground.

We walked up the field and then back to the creek. We crossed the creek and while we were standing there Happ returned. He was hot, dusty, panting. He lay down in the shallow water of the creek with his legs stretched out behind him and lapped slowly at the water.

'Happ didn't get the fox,' I said. Every time I spoke, I had the feeling I was breaking a rule of hunting, but I could not help myself. As soon as I had said this, we heard the bark of the fox again. The time it seemed closer than before. Uncle Fred shifted his gun in his hand, but he did not raise it. Happ, however, rose at once to the call, dripping wet, still panting from his last run. Nose to the ground, he headed for the trees.

The sound of his baying faded as he ran deeper into the woods. I knew the fox had nothing to fear from the hound. The fox with her light movements could run from this lumbering dog all day. It was Uncle Fred, moving closer and closer to the den with every step, who would be the end of the black fox.

to the creek, he moved into the bush.

The noise of the insects along the creek dropped into the creek again and moved up towards the thicket were standing, he could have thrown a rock over the clearing where I had seen the baby fox play

Fifteen

The Den

By this time we were only a hundred feet from the entrance to the fox's den. Uncle Fred had crossed the creek again and moved up towards the thicket of trees. From where he was standing, he could have thrown a rock over the trees and it would have landed in the little clearing where I had seen the baby fox play.

151

He walked past the thicket to a lone tree in the centre of the field and stood there for a moment. Then he knocked the creek mud on his shoe off on one of the roots and walked back to me. He turned and walked the length of the thicket. It was like that old game Hot and Cold, where you hide something and when the person gets close to it you say, 'You're getting warmer – you're warmer – now you're hot – you're red-hot – you're on fire, you're burning up!' Inside right then I was screaming, 'You're burning up.'

'Look at that,' he said. He pointed with his gun to a pile of earth that had been banked up within the last two months. 'Sometimes when a fox makes a den she'll bring the earth out one hole, seal it up, and then use the other hole for the entrance. It'll be around here somewhere.'

He moved through the trees towards the den, walking sideways. I could not move at all. I just stood with the sun beating down on my head like a fist and my nose running.

I heard the sound of Happ's barking coming closer. He had lost the fox in the woods but now he had a new scent, older, but still hot. He came crashing through the bushes, bellowing every few feet, his head to the ground. He flashed past me, not even seeing me in his intensity, his red eyes on the ground. Like a charging bull, he entered the thicket and he and Uncle Fred stepped into the small grassy clearing at the same moment.

'Here it is,' Uncle Fred called. 'Come here.'

I wanted to turn and run. I did not want to see Uncle Fred and Happ standing in that lovely secluded clearing, but instead I walked through the trees and looked at the place I had avoided so carefully for weeks. There were the bones, some whitened by the sun, a dried turkey wing, feathers, and behind, the partially sheltered hole.

Of course Uncle Fred had already seen that, and as I stepped from the trees he pointed to it with his gun.

'There's the den.'

I nodded.

'The baby foxes will be in there.'

This was the first time he had been wrong. There was only one baby fox in there, and I imagined him crouching now against the far wall of the den.

'Go back to the house and get me a shovel and sack,' Uncle Fred said.

Without speaking, I turned and walked back to the house. Behind me the black fox barked again. It was a desperate high series of barks that seemed to last a long time, and Happ lunged after the fox for the third time. It was too late now for tricks, for Uncle Fred remained, leaning on his gun waiting for the shovel and sack.

I went up the back steps and knocked. Usually

154

I just went in the house like I did at my own home, but I waited here till Aunt Millie came and I said, 'Uncle Fred wants me to bring him a sack and a shovel.'

'Did you get the fox?'

'Uncle Fred found the den.'

'If it's in the woods, he'll find it,' she said, coming out of the door, 'but you ought to see that man try to find a pair of socks in his own drawer. Hazeline,' she called up to her window, 'you want to go see your dad dig out the baby foxes?'

'No.'

'I declare that girl is in the worst mood.' She walked with me to the shed, put the shovel in my hand, and then pressed a dusty grain sack against me. 'Now, you don't be too late.'

'I don't think it will take long.'

'Are you all right? Your face is beet red.'

'I'm all right.'

'Because I can make Hazeline take that shovel to her dad.'

'I feel fine.'

I started towards the orchard with the shovel and sack and I felt like some fairy-tale character who has been sent on an impossible mission, like proving my worth by catching a thousand golden eagles in the sack and making a silver mountain for them with my shovel. Even that did not seem as difficult as what I was really doing.

It must have taken me longer to get back than I thought, for Uncle Fred said, 'I thought you'd gotten lost.'

'No, I wasn't lost. I've been here before.'

I handed him the shovel and let the sack drop to the ground. As he began to dig, I closed my eyes and pressed my hands against my eyelids, and I saw a large golden sunburst, and in this sunburst the black fox came running towards me.

I opened my eyes and watched Uncle Fred. He dug as he did everything else – powerfully, slowly, and without stopping. His shovel hit a rock and he moved the shovel until he could bring the rock out with the dirt. At my feet the gravelly pile of earth was growing.

I turned away and looked across the creek, and I saw for the fifteenth and last time the black fox. She moved anxiously towards the bushes and there was a tension to her steps, as if she were ready to spring or make some other quick, forceful movement. She barked. She had lost the dog again, and this bark was a high clear call for Uncle Fred and me to follow her.

There was a grunt of satisfaction from Uncle Fred and I turned to see him lift out, on the shovel, covered with sand and gravel, the baby fox.

He turned it on to the sack and the baby fox lay without moving.

'He's dead,' I said.

Uncle Fred shook his head. 'He's not dead. He's just play-acting. His ma taught him to do that.'

We both looked down at the little fox without speaking. I knew that if I lived to be a hundred, I would never see anything that would make me feel any worse than the sight of that little fox pretending to be dead when his heart was beating so hard it looked like it was going to burst out of his chest.

I looked over my shoulder and the black fox was gone. I knew she was still watching us, but I could not see her. Uncle Fred was probing the den with his shovel. I said, 'I don't think there are any more. She just had one.'

He dug again, piled more earth on the pile, then said, 'You're right. Usually a fox has five or six cubs.'

'I think something happened to the others.'

He bent, folded the ends of the sack, and lifted the baby fox. I took the shovel, he the gun, and we started home, the baby fox swinging between us. Happ joined us as we crossed the creek and began to leap excitedly at the sack until Uncle Fred had to hold it shoulder high to keep it from him.

We walked back to the house without speaking. Uncle Fred went directly to some old rabbit hutches beside the garage. Bubba had once raised rabbits here, but now the cages were empty. Uncle Fred opened one, shook the baby fox out of the sack, and then closed the wire door.

The baby fox moved to the back of the hutch and looked at us. His fur was soft and woolly, but his eyes were sharp. Nervously he went to one corner. Aunt Millie came out and looked. 'Just like a baby lamb,' she said. 'It's a sweet little thing, isn't it?'

'That's not the way you were talking yesterday,' Uncle Fred said.

'Well, I'm not going to have anything after my chickens,' she said. 'Not *anything*! I'd be after *you* with the broom if you bothered my chickens.' They laughed. Her spirits seemed greatly improved now that the fox was doomed, and she called, 'Hazeline, come on out here and look at this cute little baby fox.'

'No.'

Uncle Fred went into the shed, returned, and snapped a lock over the cage latch.

'You think somebody's going to steal your fox?' Aunt Millie laughed.

'I wouldn't put it past a fox to open up an unlocked cage to get her baby.'

Aunt Millie shook her head in amazement, then said, 'Well, you men have got to get washed for supper.'

We went into the house and I said to Uncle Fred, 'What are you going to do with the baby fox?'

'That's my bait. Every hunter alive's got some way to get a fox. They got some special trap or something. Mr Baynes down at the store makes up a special mixture that he says foxes can't resist. My way is to set up a trap, using the baby fox for bait. I'll sit out on the back porch tonight and watch for her.'

'Oh.'

'It never fails. That is one bait a fox can't resist.'

Sixteen

Captured

'Are you getting sick?' Aunt Millie asked at supper that night.

'I guess I'm a little tired.'

'Well, I should think so! Helping with the pump out in the boiling sun all morning and then tracking that fox all afternoon. It's a wonder you don't have heatstroke. You eat something though, hear? You have to keep up your strength.'

'I'm just not hungry.'

'It's the heat. But, listen, you drink your tea. You *will* have heatstroke sure enough if you let your body get dried out.'

I finished my tea and went up to my room. I did not even look out the window, because I knew I could see the rabbit hutch by the garage and I never wanted to see that baby fox cowering against the wall.

Hazeline came out of her room and looked in at me on the bed. 'You feeling better?'

I nodded. She was all dressed up now in a blue dress she made for 4-H. Her face looked good, as if letting it get swollen had been beneficial. I knew she was going downstairs to sit on the porch and wait for Mikey. I knew he would come, too. One time Petie and I had had the worst argument in the world. We were just sitting on the steps one afternoon and Petie had been thinking in silence for a while and then he said, 'I wonder what I'll look like when I'm grown.'

And I said, 'Porky Pig.' I don't know why I said that, because I wasn't mad at him or anything. And he said, 'Well, that's better than looking like Daffy Duck.' And I said, 'Meaning I look like Daffy Duck?' And he said, 'Yes, around the mouth.' And then we both got angry and started screaming things and I thought our friendship was over, only two days later it was just like it had never happened.

'Mikey will come over,' I said.

'Who cares? I don't care if I never see him again,' she said, twisting her fingers in her pearls. He had given her those when she had graduated from high school two months ago.

'I know, but I bet he comes anyway.'

'Well, I can't stop him of course. It's a free country.'

'Hazeline?'

'What?'

'You know that fox I was telling you about? The black one?'

'Sure.'

'Well, your dad has her baby out in the rabbit hutch and he's going to shoot her.'

'I know it. I heard. But, listen, don't let it upset you, hear?'

'Hazeline, I don't want anything to happen to that fox.'

'Tommy, listen, all wild animals die in some violent way. It's their life. Wild animals just don't die of old age. They get killed by an enemy or by the weather or they have an accident or they get rabies or some other disease or they get shot. That's the way nature is.'

'I know that,' I said quickly, because I did not want to hear any more.

'You just forget the fox. Tomorrow maybe we can go to the picture show in Clinton or something.'

'All right.'

She went down the steps then and out on to the porch, and I could hear the swing begin to creak.

I got up and went down the steps and walked to the tree in front of the rabbit hutch. I could not explain why I did this. I didn't want to see the baby fox again, and yet here I was.

He did not see me. He was busy biting the wires of his cage with great fury and determination. I could hear the clicking of his sharp tiny teeth against the wire, but he was making no progress. Then he stopped. He still had not seen me, but he had heard or smelled something and he raised his head and let out a short cry. He waited, then after a moment he began biting the wires again.

I remained by the tree watching him, listening for the quavering cry that he uttered from time to time.

'Don't get your fingers in the cage,' Uncle Fred warned behind me. 'He may not be able to cut wire yet, but he sure could hurt a finger.'

'All right.'

'In a bit, when it starts getting dark, you can sit up here with me and watch for the fox.'

A car came slowly up the drive, and I said to Uncle Fred, 'It's Mikey.'

Behind him in the doorway Aunt Millie said, 'Did you say it's Mikey, Tom?'

I nodded.

'Praise be.'

I walked around the front of the house and stood there for a minute. Mikey had not gotten out of the car but was sitting with one arm out the window, looking at Hazeline on the porch.

'What you doing?' he asked.

'Not much of anything,' she said. 'Just fighting the heat.'

'You don't look hot – you look real good and cool.'

'Sometimes looks are deceiving.'

He ran his fingers over the steering wheel. There was a pause, then he said, 'Do you want to ride up to the lake?'

'I don't know.'

'When you going to make up your mind?'

'I just don't know whether I feel like looking at boats racing all over creation tonight.'

'Do you want to go for a ride?'

'I don't know.'

'I'll give you' – he looked at his watch – 'one minute to make up your mind.'

He started watching the seconds tick off, and

I held up my watch too and counted, and only eleven seconds had gone by when Hazeline got up and said, 'I'll go,' and started laughing. 'Tell Mom I'm going off with Mikey,' she said over her shoulder and got in the car.

I went into the kitchen where Aunt Millie was standing in front of the electric fan and said, 'Hazeline has gone off with Mikey.'

I heard the cry of the baby fox again, and I thought I would be hearing that sound for ever. One time Petie Burkis fell down and broke his leg on the school playground and he said, 'Oh!' in this real terrible, painful way, and I never could forget it. Later I tried to make him say it again that same way, and one whole afternoon Petie did nothing but say the word *Oh* over and over – a thousand times maybe, and in all those thousand tries, he never sounded that same way again. I still remember it though, exactly, like

I will always remember the way that baby fox sounded when he cried.

It seemed to get dark quickly that night. Uncle Fred was already out on the back porch. He had brought out a chair and was sitting with his gun beside him, pointing to the floor. I never saw anyone sit any quieter. You wouldn't have noticed him at all he was so still.

I stood behind him inside the screen door. Through the screen I could see the tiny fox lift his black nose and cry again. Now, for the first time, there was an answer – the bark of his mother.

I looked towards the garden, because that's where the sound had come from, but Uncle Fred did not even turn his head. In a frenzy now that he had heard his mother, the baby fox moved about the cage, pulling at the wire and crying again and again.

Just then there was the sound of thunder from

the west, a long rolling sound, and Aunt Millie came to the door beside me and said, 'Bless me, is that thunder?'

She looked out at the sky. 'Was that thunder, Fred?'

'Could be,' he said without moving.

'Look!' Aunt Millie said, 'I swear I see black clouds. You see, Tom?'

'Yes'm.'

'And feel that breeze. Honestly, when you think you have reached absolutely the end of your endurance, then the breeze comes. I could not have drawn one more breath of hot air, and now we are going to have a storm.'

We stood in the doorway, feeling the breeze, forgetting for a moment the baby fox.

Then I saw Uncle Fred's gun rise ever so slightly in the direction of the fence behind the garage. I could not see any sign of the fox, but I knew that she must be there. Uncle Fred would not be wrong.

The breeze quickened, and abruptly the dishpan which Aunt Millie had left on the porch railing clattered to the floor. For the first time Uncle Fred turned his head and looked in annoyance at the pan and then at Aunt Millie.

'Did it scare your fox off?' she asked.

He nodded, then shifted in the chair and said, 'She'll be back.'

In just this short time the sky to the west had gotten black as ink. Low on the horizon forks of lightning streaked the sky.

'Now, Fred, don't you sit out here while it's thundering and lightning. I mean it. No fox is worth getting struck by lightning for.'

He nodded and she turned to me and said, 'You come on and help me shut the windows. Some of those upstairs are stuck wide open. Just hit them with the heel of your hand on the side till you can get them down.'

I started up the stairs and she said again, 'Fred, come on in when it starts storming. That fox'll be back tomorrow night too.'

I went upstairs and started hitting the sides of the windows. I had just gotten one window to jerk down about two inches when I heard the gunshot. I had never heard any worse sound in my life. It was a very final sound, like the most enormous period in the world. Bam. Period. The end.

I ran out of my room and down the steps so fast I could not even tell you how many times my feet touched the stairs, none maybe. I went out the back door, opening it so fast I hit the back of Uncle Fred's chair. I looked towards the rabbit hutch, said, 'Where?' then looked at the back fence. Then I looked down at Uncle Fred, who was doing something with his gun.

'Missed,' he said.

Suddenly I felt weak. My legs were like two pieces of rope, like that trick that Hindu magicians do when they make rope come straight up out of a basket and then say a magic word and make the rope collapse. My legs felt like they were going to collapse at any second. I managed to force these two pieces of rope to carry me up the stairs and into the room.

I closed two windows, and the third one, in sympathy perhaps, just banged down all by itself. Then I sank to the bed.

Seventeen

The Stormy Rescue

I had no intention of going to sleep when I lay down on the bed; I did not think I would ever be able to sleep again, but that is what I did. I fell right asleep and did not even move until four hours later when I awoke. It was one o'clock in the morning.

The storm was in full force, or perhaps it was a second storm, but the house was quiet. I got up and went out into the hall. I could not hear anything but the sound of the rain and Hazeline's transistor radio, which was sputtering with static beside her on the pillow.

I went down the stairs, one by one. I did not make a sound. I stepped on the part of the steps near the wall because Petie had told me that was how burglars got up stairs unheard. I was just stepping into the hall when without warning the hall light went on. Aunt Millie was standing there in her bathrobe squinting at me.

'What's wrong?' she asked.

'Nothing. I just didn't know what time it was.'

'Well' – she looked closely at her watch – 'it's just past one o'clock.'

'I went to sleep in my clothes.'

'Well, you get on your pyjamas and get back to bed. This is the first good sleeping night we've had, and you mustn't let it go to waste.'

'Sure.'

'Well, go on back up the steps.' She watched me go up two steps and then she said, 'Goodness, we've gotten on so well all summer, I'd hate for anything to happen now right before your parents get home.'

'Aunt Millie, did Uncle Fred get the fox?'

'No.'

'Is he still out on the porch?'

'In this rain? No, he is fast asleep in his bed like you ought to be.'

She waited until I was up the stairs and then she turned out the light. I went into my room and she called, 'Are you getting in bed?'

I lay down. 'Yes.'

'And go to sleep.'

I lay in bed for a long time, still in my clothes, and then I got up very carefully. I walked over to the window and looked out at the tree Bubba and

Fred Jr used to just run up and down all the time like monkeys. I could imagine them climbing up, laughing and brown, racing, going out on all sorts of perilous limbs just to be first at the window. I opened the window, pushed out the screen, reached out into the rain, and felt for the smooth spot Aunt Millie had told me was worn into the bark of the tree.

I took off my shoes and knelt on the window sill. There was an enormous flash of lightning that turned the whole world white for a moment, and then I climbed out onto the nearest branch and circled the trunk round with my arms.

I thought that I could never get one step further. I thought that I could never move even one muscle or I would fall. I thought that in the morning when Aunt Millie came up to see why I wasn't at breakfast she would find me here, pressed into the tree, still frozen with fear.

The rain was hard and slanting directly into my face. Finally I got up just enough courage to turn my face out of the rain. Then lightning flashed again and I saw the ground about a million miles below. I held the tree so tightly the bark was cutting into my cheek.

I don't know how long I stayed that way. If I had tried to look at my watch, just that little movement would have thrown me off balance. After a while, though, I began to sort of slip down the tree. I never let go of the main trunk for a second. I just moved my arms downward in very small movements. Then, slowly, when I was practically kneeling on the first limb, I let my foot reach down for the next one.

If there were smooth spots on those branches, my feet never found them. They only touched one rough limb after another as, slowly, I kept inching down the tree, feeling my way, never looking down at the ground until, finally, my foot reached out for another limb and felt the cold wet grass. It shocked me for a moment and then I jumped down, landing on my hands and knees.

I got up and ran to the rabbit hutch. The baby fox was huddled in one corner of the pen where there was some shelter from the rain. The lightning flashed and I saw him watching me.

'I'm going to get you out,' I said.

He crouched back further in the hutch. In the next flash of lightning I looked on the ground for a rock and I saw at my feet a small dead frog. I knew that the black fox in all this rain had brought that frog here to her baby. She was right now watching me somewhere.

There were bricks stacked in a neat pile under the hutch and I took one and began to bang it against the lock. I was prepared to do this all night if necessary, but the lock was an old one and it opened right away.

The noise had scared the baby fox and he was now making a whimpering sound. I unhooked the broken lock, opened the cage, and stepped back against the tree.

The baby fox did not move for a moment. I could barely see him, a small dark ball in the back of the cage. He waited, alert and suspicious, and then after a moment he moved in a crouch to the door of the cage.

He cried sharply. From the bushes there was an answering bark.

He crouched lower. The lightning flashed again and in that second he jumped and ran in the direction of the bushes. He barked as he ran. There was an immediate answer, and then only the sound of the rain. I waited against the tree, thinking about them, and then I heard the black fox bark one more time as she ran through the orchard with her baby.

And I thought, some day I will be in a famous museum, walking along on the marble floors, looking at paintings. There will be one called 'Blue Flowers' and I will look at that for a while, and the next one will be 'Woman on the Beach' and I will look at that for a while, and then I will glance at the name of the next painting and it will be 'Fox with Baby at Midnight', and I will look up and my heart will stop beating because there it will be, just the way it was this night, the black fox and her baby running beneath the wet ghostly apple trees towards a patch of light in the distance. And I thought, leaning against that tree in the rain: If there is a picture like that, I hope sometime I will get to see it.

Suddenly the rain began to slacken and I walked around the house. I had never been so wet in my life and now that it was over I was cold too. And I was tired. I looked up at the tree and there didn't seem to be any point in climbing back up when in just a few hours everyone would know what I had done anyway. I went up on the porch and rang the doorbell.

In all my life I have never felt so dumb and foolish as I did barefooted, soaking wet on that slick porch at two o'clock in the morning, waiting for someone to come and answer the door.

It was Aunt Millie in her cotton robe who turned on the porch light and peered out through the side windows at me.

I must have been an awful sight, like the poor little match girl, for she flung open the door at once and drew me in.

'What are you doing out there? What are you doing?'

'Who is it?' Uncle Fred asked as he came into the hall. He was pulling his pants up over his pyjamas.

'It's Tom,' Aunt Millie said.

'I meant who's at the door.'

'Tom,' she said again.

'Tom?'

'Yes, he was just standing out there on the porch.'

They both turned and looked at me, waiting for an explanation, and I cleared my throat and said, 'Uncle Fred and Aunt Millie, I am awfully sorry but I have let the baby fox out of the rabbit hutch.' I sounded very stiff and formal, and I thought the voice was a terrible thing to have to depend *on*, because I really did want them to know that I *was* sorry, and I didn't sound it the least bit. I knew how much Uncle Fred had looked forward to the hunt and how important getting rid of the fox was to Aunt Millie, and I hated for them to be disappointed now.

There was a moment of silence. Then Aunt

Millie said, 'Why, that's perfectly all right, isn't it, Fred? Don't you think another thing about that. You just come on to bed. You're going to get pneumonia standing there in that puddle.' She started for the linen closet. 'I'll get you some towels.'

Uncle Fred and I were left in the hall alone and I looked up at him and he looked like an enormous blue-eyed Indian.

'I'm sorry,' I said again.

He looked at me and I knew he was seeing through all the very casual questions I had been asking all summer about foxes, and seeing through the long days I had spent in the woods. He was remembering the sorry way I had tried to keep him from finding the fox's den and the way I had looked when we did find it. I think all those pieces just snapped into place right then in Uncle Fred's mind and I knew that if there was

185

one person in the world who understood me it was this man who had seemed such a stranger.

He cleared his throat. 'I never liked to see wild things in a pen myself,' he said.

Aunt Millie came down the hall and threw a towel over my head and started rubbing. 'Now get upstairs. I am not going to have you lying in bed with pneumonia when your mother arrives.'

We went upstairs, she rubbing my head the whole way, me stumbling over the steps, and Hazeline calling from her room, 'Who was that at the door?'

'Tom,' Aunt Millie said.

'Who?'

'Me,' I said.

'Oh.'

We went into my room. 'There,' Aunt Millie exclaimed at the sight of my open window, 'I knew it! I knew you'd be out there on that tree at the first opportunity.' She shut the window with a bang. 'There is no explaining a boy.'

She turned down my bed, went out, and came back with a glass of milk.

'I'm sorry about your turkey and hen,' I said.

'Oh, that! I bet you think I'm awful, carrying on the way I did.'

'No.'

'It was more the heat than anything else, like Fred said. Just don't think about it any more. That fox and her baby are miles away from here now, and they'll never come back to bother my birds. That's one thing about a fox. He learns.'

She turned out the light, said, 'It is starting to rain again. I declare we are going to be flooded out,' and then went downstairs.

Eighteen
Goodbye

The next week I spent in the woods, assuring myself that the black fox had gone. I sat on the rock over the ravine, I lay by the creek, I went back to the den again and again to look at the ruins, I sat by the field where the mice ran. I never once saw or heard the black fox and I knew I never would again.

While I was making my last trip through the

woods – a great double-clover-leaf walk that covered the entire forest – my parents came driving up to the farm. I had not expected them that day but they were so eager to see me – they told me this later – that they had got in the car practically as soon as they got home and set off for the farm.

I was up the creek having one more look at the old ruined den when I heard this honking coming from near the house. The honking stopped and even though I couldn't hear him I knew that it was my father and that he was now saying, 'Anybody home?'

I ran down the creek and through the orchard, and my mom had come around to the back of the house looking for me. She grabbed me and said, 'Oh, you look so good,' and, 'You are the tallest thing I ever saw,' and to Dad, 'Look, we have a giant for a son now.' Dad came over and punched me on the arm and said, 'How are you, sport?'

'I'm fine, Dad.'

'Look who we brought with us.'

I looked and there was Petie Burkis, and I knew suddenly why I looked so different and tall to my parents, because that was the way Petie looked to me.

'Hi, Petie.'

'Hi,' he said.

He came over and said, 'Well, I bet you're surprised to see me.'

'I didn't know you were coming.'

'I know.'

'You take Petie around and show him the farm if you want to,' Aunt Millie said to me, then to Mom, 'Honestly, that boy of yours has not given me one minute of trouble the whole summer. Come on in the house. He has just been *wonderful*.'

They went into the house and I hoped that Aunt Millie was not going to tell about my climbing out the window and down that tree, because the way she would tell it, I would sound like Tom Sawyer, and Mom and Dad would get a great false hope that I had in one summer suddenly changed into an athlete.

'This doesn't look too bad for a farm,' Petie was saying.

'No, it's not too bad.'

'I bet you had fun out here.'

'It was all right.'

'I wouldn't mind spending a whole summer out here. I really wouldn't.' He fell in beside me as we walked to the barn. 'It would be better than being home. There wasn't anything but re-runs on TV all summer.'

'Those are Uncle Fred's pigs down there. The big one got some sort of prize.'

In silence we stopped and looked at the pigs. Then Petie said, 'Hey, you know what happened?'

'What?'

'Teddy Wilson – that big boy with the silver bicycle – broke his leg.'

'I didn't know that.'

'And you know that girl that sat in the front of our room in maths?'

'Mary McGee?'

'Yes. Well, she accidentally started her father's car and wrecked into a tree.'

Then we were silent again. It was a funny thing – I could have gone into the house right then and written Petie a five-page letter about all kinds of things, but I couldn't think of anything to say.

'Boy, they sure have got some sickening commercials on TV though,' Petie said. 'They have this one for corns and calluses where they show this plastic foot with these fake, lift-out corns. It would make you sick.'

'What else do they have?'

'They have this one about room deodorants. It's

real sickening. It has a kitchen that looks like it smells bad, and then it shows this woman coming into the kitchen and a man's voice says, "It's a scientific fact that you can get used to any smell in 151 seconds, only why bother?" And then this hand comes out and sprays room deodorant everywhere.'

'You believe that about the 151 seconds?'

'I don't believe it,' Petie said. 'That's just what the commercial says.'

'We could test it. I've got my watch.'

Suddenly Petie looked like himself again. He was rubbing his hands up and down his shirt, which is what he always does when he gets enthusiastic about something.

'Where is the worst smell on this whole farm?' he said. 'The very worst?'

'Come on.'

'And, listen,' he continued, 'if it doesn't work, I will write them a letter – very business-like – and say something like this. "Gentlemen: Contrary to your scientific fact, my friend –" No, make that, "my *partner* and I have tested a wide variety of smells. Our discoveries are below." '

Nineteen

A Memory

We left the farm after breakfast the next morning. Aunt Millie and Uncle Fred were by the car, and Hazeline was saying, 'Now you come back on the thirtieth to my wedding, you hear? All of you!'

'We will if we possibly can,' my mom said. 'I still cannot believe that you are getting married, because the last time I saw you, you know, you were in pigtails.'

'We'd better get going,' Dad said. 'The traffic's going to be bad.'

'Well, at least we won't be on bicycles,' Mom said. 'I couldn't pedal from here to the porch if my life depended on it.'

Dad put my suitcase and Petie's in the back seat and shook hands with Uncle Fred. I hated to say goodbye to people I liked. Nothing made me feel worse.

Mom hugged Aunt Millie and Uncle Fred and then they all looked at me, and right then I wanted to say the greatest thing in the world to Aunt Millie and Uncle Fred, because I had realised after I let the fox go that they were probably the nicest people I would ever meet. In all the past week they had never mentioned once what I had done.

All I could say though was, 'Aunt Millie, I will

never, ever forget how good it was to be on the farm with you and Uncle Fred.'

'Well, it's just been real good for us to have you,' she said. She hugged me and kissed me on my eyebrow.

Uncle Fred said, 'You come back next summer. Send the folks to Australia or somewhere.'

'Only *please* not on bicycles,' Mom said.

We all laughed and got in the car and Petie Burkis said, 'Thank you for having me,' in an odd voice.

'You come back, too, Petie,' Aunt Millie said.

'I will.'

Then Aunt Millie and Uncle Fred and Hazeline stepped back from the car and we drove off. Dad started blowing the horn and said, 'Home, here we come.'

I looked back all the way to the main road, because you could get a real good view of the whole farm, and I wanted to memorise it. Aunt Millie was still waving, but Hazeline had sat down on the steps and was saying something to her dad.

'Well, how will it be to get home, Tom?' my dad said.

'Real good, I guess.'

'To tell you the truth, our old house looked better to me than any castle I saw in Europe.'

Mom turned around and smiled and said, 'Now, tell me, how was the farm really?'

'It wasn't bad.'

'I told you, didn't I? I told you you'd like it.'

'I loved it,' I said. It was the first time I had ever admitted that my parents were right about something and I was wrong, and this made her feel enormously good and she said again, 'I knew you would.'

It was afternoon when we got home and everything was just the same, our street, the house, everything. The only thing that seemed the least bit different to me was when I went in my room, because all I could see at first was models, models, hundreds of models everywhere. You would have thought that I had done nothing all my life but glue pieces of plastic together. That was funny, too, because when I was at the farm remembering my room, I had never thought once about all these models.

The rest of the summer went by so quickly that it was like the whole summer had been spent on the farm, because Petie and I hardly had time to do anything before school started. Then we joined a science club that met every Saturday, and the whole year just started flying by. I never knew time could go so fast.

And pretty soon my visit to the farm began to seem hazy. For one thing I couldn't remember the way Aunt Millie and Uncle Fred and Hazeline looked. Hazeline had sent me a picture of her feeding wedding cake to Mikey with Aunt Millie and Uncle Fred standing beside them, but they certainly hadn't looked like that, all stiff and formal and in clothes that seemed to have been made for other people. Only I couldn't remember exactly what they had looked like.

And one night I tried to think of the name of Uncle Fred's prize pig. I must have heard him say her name a thousand times that summer, only I had to lie in my bed for about three hours before I finally remembered that it was Rowina.

It all seemed like something that had happened to another boy instead of me. Like one time Petie and I made a time capsule out of a large jar, and we put into this jar all kinds of things, so that in a hundred years, or a thousand, someone would find this capsule, open it, and know exactly what Petie Burkis and I had been like. We put pictures of ourselves in the jar and lists of things we had done and Petie wrote down everything he ate and drank in one day and I wrote down the books I had read in the past year. We put in stories we had written about our families for English class and Petie's poem 'TV Land' and pictures we had drawn, and then we buried it. A year went by and one day Petie said, 'Hey, let's go dig up the time capsule.' So we ran and dug it up and took all the stuff out and laid it on the ground and read it and Petie kept saying, 'I never wrote that. I *know* I never wrote that.' And I was the same way about this crayon picture with my name on it. I couldn't remember doing it at all. It was as if two other boys had made up the time capsule and buried it in the ground. And now, that was the way I felt about the farm. It was as if it had happened to another boy, not me at all.

But then sometimes at night, when the rain is

beating against the windows of my room, I think about that summer and everything is crystal clear. I am once again beside the creek. The air is clean and the grass is deep and very green. And I look up and see the black fox leaping over the crest of the hill and she is exactly as she was the first time I saw her.

Or I am beneath that tree again. The cold rain is beating down upon me and my heart is in my throat.

And I hear, just as plainly as I heard it that August night, above the rain, beyond the years, the high clear bark of the midnight fox.